ghost

Thirteen Haunting Tales to Tell

A collection by *illustratus*

chronicle books

san francisco

This book is dedicated to those who face their fears.

Text and illustrations copyright © 2019 by Illustrátus.

Library of Congress Cataloging-in-Publication Data:

Names: Hemingway, Blaise, author. | Reffsin, Jesse, author. | Sasaki, Chris, illustrator. | Turley, Jeff (Illustrator), illustrator.

Title: Ghost / Blaise Hemingway, Jesse Reffsin ; [illustrated by Chris Sasaki and Jeff Turley]

Description: San Francisco, CA : Chronicle Books, [2019] | Summary: A collection of thirteen original ghost stories, some in rhyme, by Blaise Hemingway and Jesse Reffsin, accompanied by illustrations by Chris Sasaki and Jeff Turley.

Identifiers: LCCN 2017061556 | ISBN 9781452171289 (alk. paper)

Subjects: LCSH: Ghost stories. | Horror tales. | Stories in rhyme. | CYAC: Ghosts--Fiction. | Horror stories. | Short stories. | LCGFT: Horror fiction.

Classification: LCC PZ5.H3595 Gh 2019 | DDC [Fic]--dc23 LC record available at https://lccn.loc.gov/2017061556

Manufactured in China.

Design by Alice Seiler.
Typeset in Baskerville.
The illustrations in this book were rendered digitally.

10 9 8 7 6 5 4 3 2 1

Chronicle Books LLC
680 Second Street
San Francisco, California 94107

Chronicle Books—we see things differently. Become part of our community at www.chroniclekids.com.

thank you

We would like to thank all those who
believed in us and the idea behind *Ghost*.
Working on this book has been a true
pleasure and we hope you enjoy reading
it as much as we did creating it.

prologue

Written by Blaise Hemingway
Illustrated by Jeff Turley

Prologue

It was in the mess hall that the boys first heard about Camp Champlain's groundskeeper, Old Man Blackwood.

Blackwood lived in a one-room cabin at the southern edge of the camp property, in the marshlands near the abandoned highway. The rumor was that Blackwood knew all the best ghost stories, the ones that were too scary or too gruesome for the counselors to tell the young campers around the campfire.

Thomas was too scared to try to find Blackwood's cabin alone, in the dark, but when his bunkmate Skeeter announced he was going to make the long walk across the marsh that night, Thomas said, "I'll come, too." But the words had no sooner left his lips than Thomas found himself consumed with dread.

After that evening's last bunk check, and Skeeter snuck out of their beds, the camp's gravel road to the derelict then hopped a split rail fence into the marsh, on the other side of which sat wood's cabin.

Trudging through the marsh, the boys shoes sink into the mud deeper and de they swatted away the waist-high grass seemed to grow higher with every step ground beneath them was soft, so soft if you stood still for too long—you'd si into it. Thomas looked around and rea he couldn't tell which way they'd come

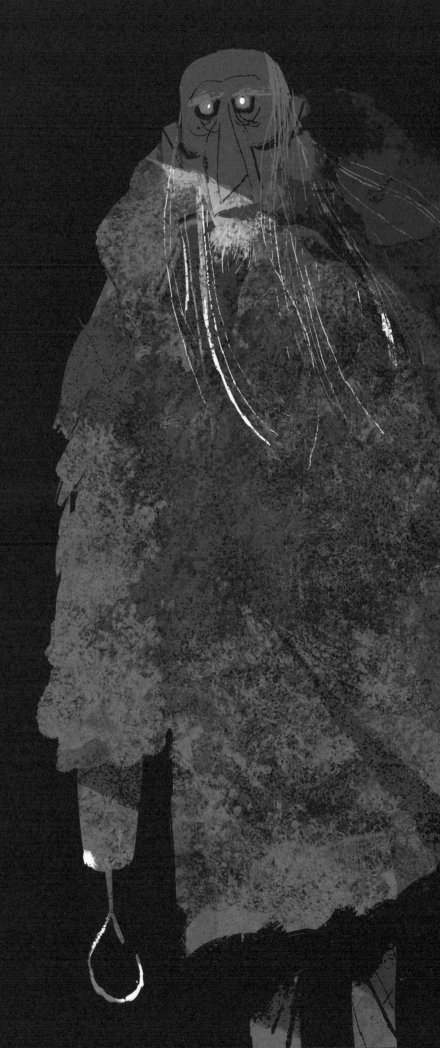

"What if we get caught?" whispered Thomas nervously.

"We're not gonna get caught," said Skeeter, as he marched confidently ahead. "And you don't have to whisper. Go on and scream if you want. Nobody can hear us."

Thomas gulped. The fact that no one could hear them made the boy even *more* nervous.

The boys walked for what seemed like hours. Tired and muddy, Thomas became certain that they would never find their way out of the marsh, but just as it seemed he could not take another step, Skeeter pointed through the trees, exclaiming, "Look!"

The full moon illuminated Old Man Blackwood's cabin, a decrepit, crumbling structure. The wooden planks were dried and cracking; the tin roof was rusted with holes. The foundation was sinking into the swampy earth below, so much so that the cabin tilted slightly on the right side. Though Thomas had never laid eyes on it before, there was something very familiar about the rickety old home.

Skeeter rapped his knuckles against the cabin's door. The boys waited, but there was no response and they heard no one stirring inside.

"Too bad!" said Thomas. "He's not home. I guess we should head back to camp, huh?" But just as he said it, the door swung open.

Standing in the doorway was an old man with long, thin, grey hair, a splotchy, bristly beard, and—hanging from his right elbow—a flesh-colored prosthetic arm and hook.

Thomas held his breath as Old Man Blackwood stared down at him, both eyes clouded over with cataracts. After what felt like an eternity, the man said with a sneer, "You've come for the stories?"

Thomas somehow managed to nod. Old Man Blackwood snorted and then walked back into the cabin, leaving the door open behind him.

Thomas turned to Skeeter, seeing for the first time that his friend was now as scared as he. But before Thomas could suggest that they both run, Blackwood snapped at them, "Hurry up. And don't forget to shut the door behind you. Yer letting in a draft."

The interior of the cabin was dimly lit by a single hanging gas lantern. The walls were covered with the dried skins of squirrels and rabbits. Deer antlers hung from the ceiling, suspended by thin strands of animal sinew. The room smelled sour with the rotting flesh of dead things.

The chair creaked loudly as Old Man Blackwood lowered himself into it, taking a seat at a small table in the center of the cabin. He picked up a tin cup and spit tobacco juice into it. Thomas watched, disgusted, as Blackwood wiped brown saliva from his lips with the sleeve of his torn flannel shirt.

The grizzled groundskeeper nodded to two open seats at the table. Thomas started to move toward a chair, before noticing that Skeeter had remained motionless, too paralyzed by fright to do anything. Thomas grabbed him by the arm and pulled him into a seat.

"There are only thirteen *true* ghost stories in this world." Blackwood shifted, leaning forward in his chair, the candlelight reflected in his smoky eyes. "*Tonight*, I'm gonna tell you them *all*."

reflection

Written by Jesse Reffsin
Illustrated by Chris Sasaki

Reflection

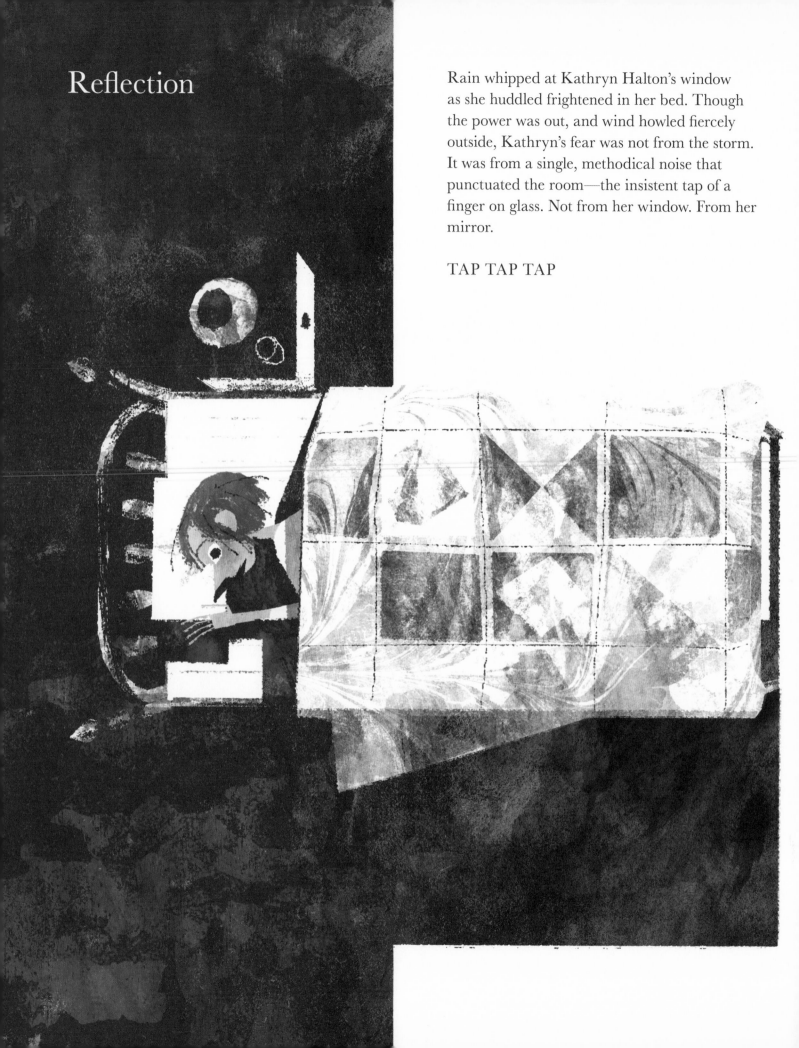

Rain whipped at Kathryn Halton's window as she huddled frightened in her bed. Though the power was out, and wind howled fiercely outside, Kathryn's fear was not from the storm. It was from a single, methodical noise that punctuated the room—the insistent tap of a finger on glass. Not from her window. From her mirror.

TAP TAP TAP

The room was dark, but there was just enough light for Kathryn to distinguish the gleam of the looking glass across the room. There, she could make out faint movement. Just her reflection.

She reached for the glass on her nightstand, hoping the water would calm her shaky nerves. But at that same instant, a crack of lightning filled the sky. In the momentary flash, Kathryn caught a glimpse of her reflection, this time glaring out from the surface of the glass, its grin stretched wide with malice.

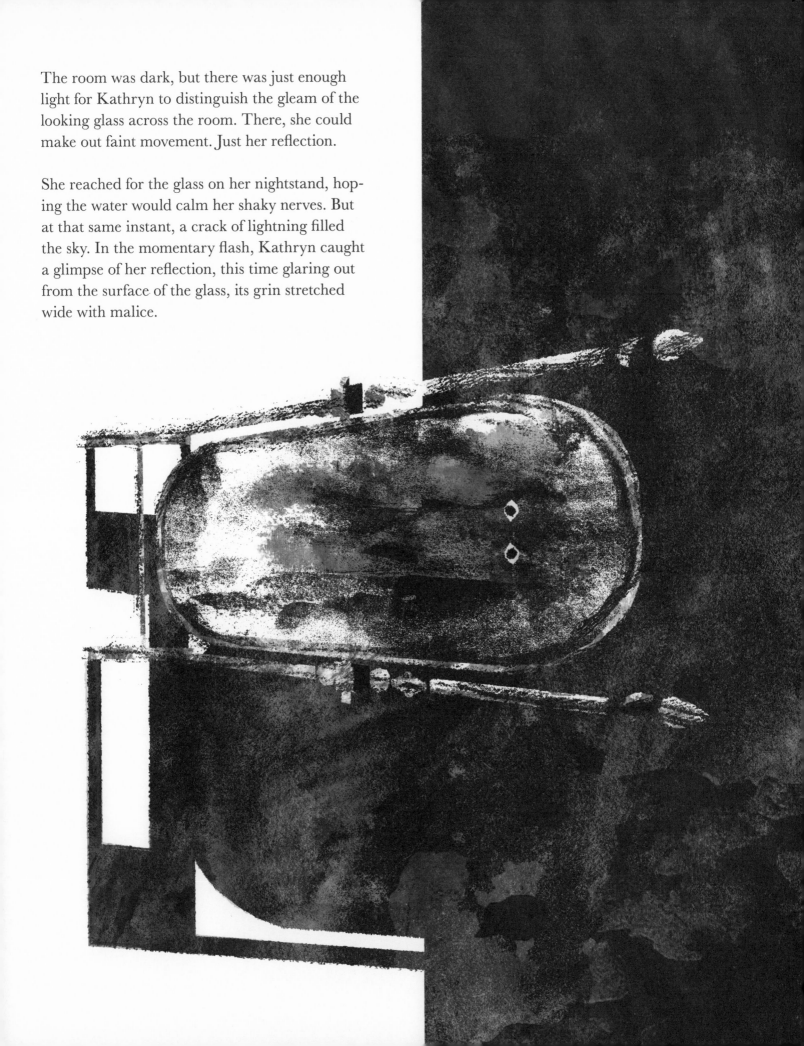

Kathryn dropped the glass in fright. It shattered against the room's aged oak floorboards, and water cut a jagged puddle across the floor, dark as blood in the dim room.

Kathryn silently cursed as she ran to her bathroom for a towel. She was careful to avoid the bathroom mirror, but she couldn't help catching the erratic movement of her reflection in the corner of her eye, beckoning her to look back.

As she hurried to her bed, the same insistent tapping followed her from the bathroom.

TAP TAP TAP

Kathryn moved quickly to sop up the spill, but even here she found her reflection staring back menacingly from the dark pool of water. Kathryn tossed the towel down to cover it.

She'd never before realized how unavoidable her own reflection was—mirrors, glass, water. There was no escape from the dark double, wordlessly stalking her while the storm raged outside.

What did it want?

TAP TAP TAP

The noise floated to Kathryn across the deep shadows of the room in response. There was no way around it. She took a deep breath and looked up at the full-length mirror opposite her bed. Her reflection loomed in the glass, almost ghostly pale in the dim moonlight. It crooked a finger at her, motioning her over.

It dawned on Kathryn that the only peace she'd find that night would be in doing as it wanted. She walked slowly across the room. The floorboards creaked under her weight. The storm pelted the window in a torrent of rain.

Up close, Kathryn's reflection was identical to her, except for the sinister look on its face. It was deeply unnerving. Kathryn thought of all the times she'd examined her reflection, unaware that it might be staring back at her.

The reflection brought her back from the unsettling train of thought as it pantomimed touching its finger to the glass. It wanted her to tap the mirror.

At Kathryn's hesitation, a clap of thunder drew her attention to the window. Her reflection was there as well, staring out from the glass pane, a reminder that there was no escape.

Kathryn made up her mind and slowly raised her trembling hand. The reflection nodded approvingly as Kathryn's finger struck the cold mirror.

TAP

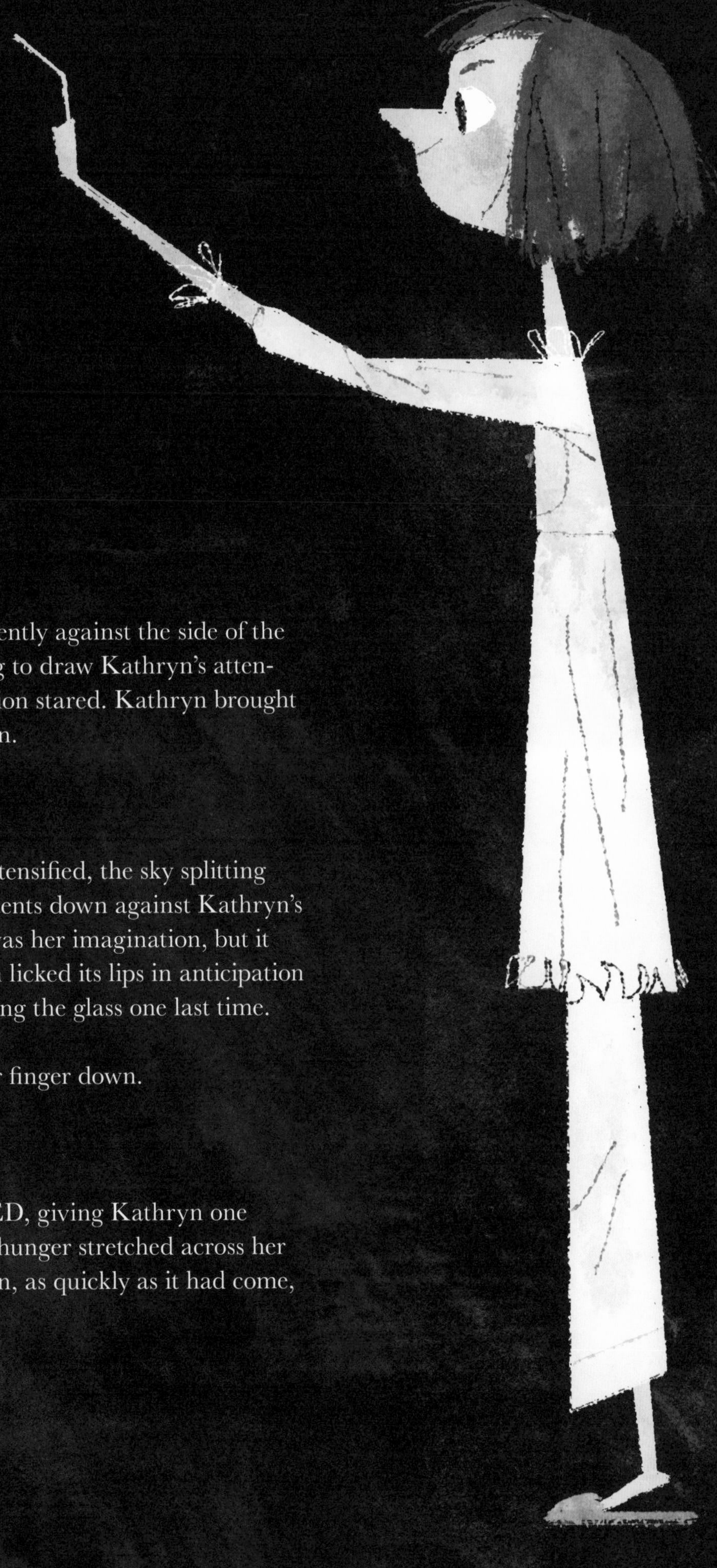

Wind pounded insistently against the side of the old house, as if trying to draw Kathryn's attention, too. The reflection stared. Kathryn brought her finger down again.

TAP

The storm outside intensified, the sky splitting wide to bleed its contents down against Kathryn's window. Perhaps it was her imagination, but it seemed her reflection licked its lips in anticipation of her finger contacting the glass one last time.

Kathryn brought her finger down.

TAP

Lightning CRACKED, giving Kathryn one last look at the deep hunger stretched across her reflection's face. Then, as quickly as it had come, the light vanished.

The next morning the rain had given way to
sunlight, now filtering warmly into the room.
A slender, brown-haired girl slept peacefully in
the bed. But Kathryn, hoarse from screaming
through the long, dark night, was not at rest.

Though her fists were bruised and bloodied,
she pounded hopelessly on the thick surface of
the mirror. No matter how she tried, she could
produce only the slightest noise in the world
beyond the glass.

TAP TAP TAP

the old pond

Written by Blaise Hemingway
as told by Scott Turley

The Old Pond

Samuel picked at his food, the sharp sound of fork scraping porcelain echoing in the small kitchen. Dinner was a silent affair. The boy's parents rarely spoke these days. Then again, they didn't have to; the signs of grieving carved deeply into their faces did all the talking for them.

Though two years his junior, Emily had been in the same grade as Samuel. The year he was held back, Emily skipped, so Samuel had to suffer the humiliation of repeating the fourth grade in his little sister's class. School—like everything else in Emily's life—had come easy for her. Emily was smart. She was beautiful. She was popular. And she never hesitated to remind Samuel that *he* was none of those things. Emily teased Samuel both day and night, at school and home, in front of friends and family, always finding new ways to embarrass him.

But there was *one* place where Samuel could escape his sister's taunting. One place where Emily floundered and Samuel thrived. *The old pond*. While Samuel would swim every day until winter's chill froze the pond over, Emily kept her distance. Not a strong swimmer, Emily never ventured deeper than into waist-high water.

But that was what made her drowning so suspect. What possessed Emily to swim out to the deepest part of the old pond? What was she thinking? *Why would she do it?* The question lingered.

Samuel excused himself from the table and went upstairs, climbing beneath the woolen covers of his bed. As he laid his head to the pillow, Samuel turned to the large window facing the backyard. Through it, the boy could see the moon reflecting on the still water of the old pond, the same way it had the night Emily drowned. The boy shivered, trying to push that horrible memory away. Samuel turned to face the ceiling, holding his stare on it until his eyelids finally grew heavy and he slowly drifted to sleep.

It was the sound of splashing that startled Samuel awake. His eyes sprang open and he looked out his window. Ripples of water broke up reflected moonlight on the old pond. Something . . . or *someone* . . . was in there.

Curious, Samuel rose from his bed, stumbled down the stairs, and stepped out the back door of the house. A thin mist clawed out of the water toward the boy, forming a path that led Samuel right to the old pond.

Samuel slowly walked toward the silent water, over the dew-covered grass that wet his bare feet and the cuffs of his pajama pants. Samuel stopped at the shoreline, watching and listening carefully, but . . . the splashing had stopped. The old pond was quiet and perfectly still.

Samuel turned to look back at the house—and *the splashing started again.* Samuel slowly craned his head around and spotted ripples in the water.

"Hello?" the boy called out, his voice cracking. "Is someone out there?"

"Help me! Help me, Samuel!"

He immediately recognized the voice crying out to him.

"Emily?" The boy squinted, scanning the surface of the pond.

"Please, Samuel! Help me!" His sister called to him, voice gurgling as her throat filled with water.

Samuel looked far out to the center of the pond where he could faintly see his sister, bobbing up and down, flailing and grasping desperately at the surface of the water.

Instinct took over. Samuel dove into the pond, swimming as quickly as his arms could carry him, stealing glimpses at his struggling sister, making certain she was still there.

"I've got you! I've got you!"

Samuel wrapped his arms around Emily as she coughed up pond water and gasped. She was shaken, but alive.

Tears rolled down Samuel's face as he gripped tightly to his little sister.

"Everything's gonna be okay, Emily. Everything's okay," said the boy with relief.

Samuel started to swim for shore, towing Emily behind him. With every stroke, the guilt the boy had carried for months began to dissipate. *He* had been the one to dare Emily to swim to the middle of the pond. He'd only wanted to see Emily struggle at something, the same way he had struggled with so many other things in his life. Samuel never anticipated that she would drown. But now he was given this second chance.

He continued to swim, but his strokes became slower, and *slower*. Samuel's muscles ached. His breathing was strained. Despite his best efforts, he didn't seem to be moving. He was stuck in the dead center of the old pond.

Samuel turned to see if he and Emily were caught on something. It was only then that he actually looked at his sister's face, now fully illumined by the light of the moon.

Emily's skin was pale, almost translucent. Raised black veins traced her face and neck. Her eyes were black, and lifeless.

"Emily?"

Emily's mouth curled into a maleficent grin, revealing two rows of long pointed teeth.

With a violent jerk, Samuel was plunged below the water, pulled with a force that he had no chance of resisting. He screamed and flailed, fighting against it with all his might, desperately trying to make his way back to the surface, but he could not.

Samuel watched helplessly as the moon's reflection became smaller and smaller while he sunk deeper and deeper. Finally the moon disappeared from his sight completely. As the last bubble of air left his lips, he knew he would never again return from the black depths of the old pond.

the doll

Written by Jesse Reffsin
Illustrated by Chris Sasaki

The Doll

The girl walked through the storefront door.
Its antique bell gave ring.
Her mother frowned, close behind.
"Don't you touch a thing."

The girl sighed and rolled her eyes.
She'd heard that one before.
Her mother always told her no
when entering a store.

Her mother's favorite thing to say
was *no*, or *don't*, or *stop*.
The words were ready on her lips
at first sight of the shop.

As usual, this trip was meant
for Mother's wants alone.
She'd never think to buy her "brat"
a present of her own.

Though once inside, it mattered not,
for looking 'round that store,
she'd found it only full of junk.
Trash, and nothing more.

But where the mother saw the bad,
her daughter saw the good.
Tucked amongst the rundown shelves
sat a doll—made out of wood.

The girl stopped, full of wonder,
at the doll's hand-painted face.
She didn't mind its lack of hair
or dislike its tattered lace.

She plucked the doll from off the shelf,
its smile cheap and gaudy.
"Mother, may I have this doll?"
"Over my dead body."

The girl was scolded for what Mother called
a total lack of taste.
A horrid doll, a horrid girl.
To buy it? "What a waste!"

The mother showed her own blonde hair
and dress with pale plaid print,
as two examples of true beauty,
of which the doll bore not a hint.

The girl had no recourse,
there was nothing she could say.
Her mother's mind was set in stone,
so they went on their way.

Back at home, the girl's bedroom
stood just off the hall.
And there she found, wrapped in a box,
the gaudy, hairless doll.

She looked around and puzzled how
the doll had come to be
in her room despite the fact
her mother had not agreed.

But soon the worry left her,
and to a smile it gave way.
The doll was now hers to have.
Her mother had no say.

To her delight, she also found
some trimmings that came with it:
a blonde-haired wig to change its look.
A pale plaid dress to fit it.

She dressed the doll and placed its wig,
and prized it like no other.
But oddly enough, in dress and wig,
it looked quite like her mother.

The difference was the doll could not
say *stop* or *don't* or *no*.
In fact the doll spoke not at all.
The girl did love it so.

And perhaps it did look horrid,
that doll in pale plaid prints,
But the girl heard no more about it,
for she hadn't seen her mother since.

point whitney

Written by Blaise Hemingway
Illustrated by Jeff Turley

Point Whitney

The deafening hum of his snowmobile rang in Max's ears. Across the frozen lake to his right were dotted hundreds of multicolored shacks of varying shapes and sizes. *Ice shanties*, he remembered hearing the locals calling them, shelters to protect the ice fishermen from the winds that came in from the west and sped with a piercing chill over the lake.

Ahead, Max noticed Tyler's brake lights glowing. The older boy's snowmobile stopped at a small shop off the country road that ran the perimeter of the lake. A wooden sign hanging from its porch read: *Whitney's Bait & Tackle*.

The bell tied to the door rang as Max followed Tyler into the shop. Tyler marched to the refrigerators in the back of the store, whose shelves were piled high with Styrofoam containers of black soil and squirming earthworms.

To the left of the refrigerators, Max saw an old, framed photograph of a man mounted to the wall. The man in the picture looked like the kind who thrived in these harsh New England winters. He was tall, bulky, and stoic. His index and middle fingers were hooked deep into the gills of a gigantic fish that stretched nearly the entire length of the man's body. Large chunks of bloody fish innards were frozen to his jacket sleeve. If Max didn't know better, he'd have thought the man in the photograph was staring right at him.

"That's Charlie Whitney," called out the elderly shopkeeper to Max. "This used to be his shop, 'fore he fell through the ice." Max's eyes went wide and he turned to face the shopkeeper, who was now pointing out the window at a barren peninsula jutting into the lake. "He was fishing north of the point. Went through the ice and never came up."

With a gulp, Max asked, "They *never* found him?"

The shopkeeper shook his head. "He's still out there. On a quiet night, you can hear Charlie Whitney's boots crunching against the ice. That's why no one fishes north of Point Whitney anymore. Them fish belong to *him*." The shopkeeper looked up at Max, who could feel the hairs on the back of his neck rising.

Tyler rolled his eyes as he set three containers of earthworms on the counter. "Nine dollars," said the shopkeeper and placed them into a large brown paper bag, the containers making a shrill sound as they rubbed against each other.

Tyler threw the money on the counter, took the bag, and pushed open the door. He turned to Max impatiently. "Well? You coming or aren't you?"

Max mumbled a thank-you and turned to go. The shopkeeper leaned over the counter and grabbed Max's arm. "Don't go north of the point." He stared intensely at Max. *"Them are Charlie's fish."*

Max could see the shopkeeper's heavy lower eyelids hanging slack under his spider-webbed, bloodshot eyes. He felt a nervous pang in his stomach and squirmed out of the shopkeeper's grip, scurrying through the door to catch up with Tyler, who was already on his snowmobile, heading toward the frozen shore.

The boys had to slow as they drove out onto the frozen lake, the engines quiet enough to hear the muffled cracking of ice below. Max shivered, though not from the cold.

They closed in on the makeshift village of ice shanties in the bay of the lake. Max passed fishermen by the dozens in frosted-over orange snowsuits, densely packed and huddled over small holes in the ice. The men looked as if they'd been waiting an eternity to make their catch, but their buckets were empty, not a fish to be seen.

"Screw this," said Tyler as he revved his engine, turned left, and sped away from the shanties. Though confused, Max followed Tyler north, straight for the peninsula the shopkeeper had told them to avoid, the ominous point where Charlie Whitney had fallen through the ice to his death.

When Tyler finally stopped and parked at the tip of the point, Max looked back at the shanties that were now just specks in the white distance. "We're fishing *here?*" asked Max uneasily.

"There's too many people in the bay," snapped back the older boy as he removed the bungee cords holding a large gas-powered drill to the back of his snowmobile. "We'll catch way more fish here."

Tyler violently yanked on the starter rope on the drill to get it spinning. Max watched as Tyler jammed the drill into the ice, quickly chewing through the layers of frozen lake. It wasn't long before Max heard the drill break through underneath.

"But the guy at the tackle shop said we weren't supposed to go north of Point Whitney," Max protested.

Tyler grabbed a squirming earthworm from a Styrofoam container and jammed the hook of his fishing line into it. "I don't care what he said. My dad says that old man's nuts."

Tyler pulled a milk crate to the edge of the hole, sat on it, and then cast his line in. Max stood unmoving for a long while, contemplating what to do.

"You're such a freakin' baby," said Tyler disgustedly. "I can't wait to tell everyone at school that you were scared of some stupid frozen fisherman." Max got enough grief from the boys back at St. Andrews; he didn't need more. He baited his hook, cast his line, and waited.

Max was scanning the frozen lake, watching swirling wisps of snow float past, when he heard the sloshing of water. Tyler yelped with joy as he pulled a flailing fish from his hole in the ice.

Tyler proudly tossed his prize into a five-gallon bucket of water, where it continued to thrash. The older boy looked up at Max with a self-satisfied smile. "What'd I tell you? This is the spot."

Tyler was right. Soon the boys filled their bucket to the brim with trout and pike. As the sun started to set, they sealed the top of the bucket and lashed it to Tyler's snowmobile.

Max hurried to get his snowmobile started as the inches of snow quickly accumulated around Point Whitney. While Max fumbled with his ignition, Tyler took off. The older boy sped over the ice, laughing. Tyler had been coming to this lake his whole life and knew it well, but this was Max's first time, and he was less than certain how to find his way back. Max shouted, "Wait up!" as the snow flurries began to fall more thickly.

Finally, his chilly engine roared to life. Max put the sled into drive and took off, hoping to catch up with Tyler before full dark.

But Tyler's tracks disappeared beneath the freshly fallen show, which was now coming down hard. Max cursed himself for not wearing goggles as snowflakes pelted his face, his lashes becoming so laden with ice that his eyelids stuck together.

Just as the fear that he would never find his way off this frozen lake started to overcome him, Max saw the red brake lights of Tyler's snowmobile in the distance. Max twisted the accelerator and drove as fast as he could to catch up.

He was surprised by how quickly he was able to close the gap between him and his companion, but—as Tyler's snowmobile came into full view—Max saw that it was parked . . . and Tyler was nowhere to be seen.

"Tyler!" Max stopped the snowmobile and ran, frantically shouting the older boy's name as the winds howled. In his panic, Max lost his footing on the snow-slicked ice and fell, his face smashing hard against it. He tasted something warm and metallic filling his mouth. He spit, seeing his two front teeth and blood splatter in the snow.

As Max wiped the blood from his lips, he heard a scratching sound and a muffled scream coming from *beneath* the ice. Max dragged his body closer to the sound and then started digging through the snow, pushing the thick powder away from the frozen lake.

As Max swept away the last bit of snow from the ice, he found himself staring at someone trapped inside it. *It was Tyler,* his body fully encased under two feet of frozen lake water as he clawed and scratched, trying to get out. The panic-stricken older boy screamed for Max to help him.

Max banged against the ice as hard as he could until the knuckles inside his gloves were raw and bloody. But the boy's efforts were in vain. Max watched helplessly as Tyler's skin turned blue and his mouth froze, twisted and open in mid-scream.

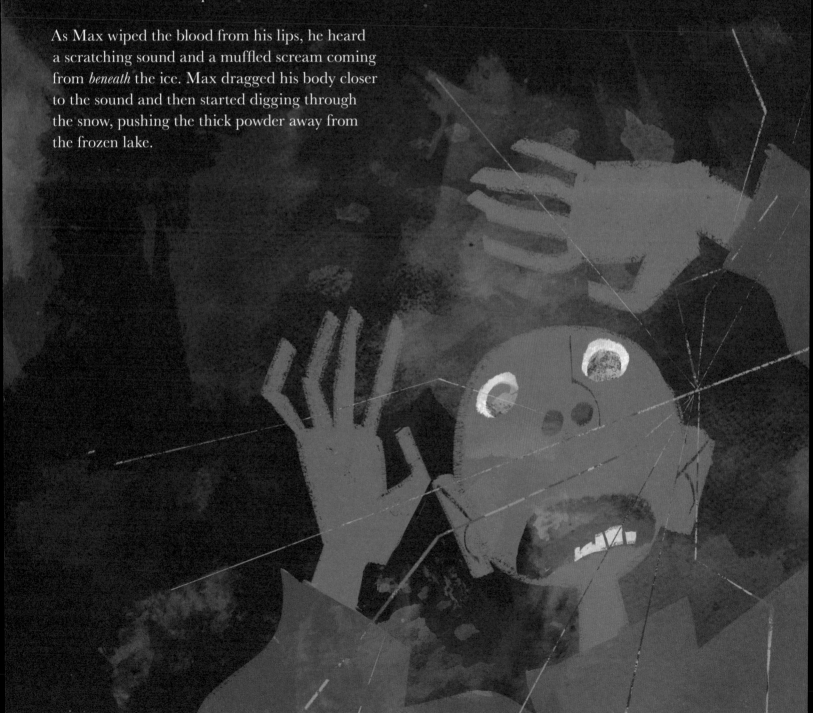

Max now felt his own body freezing solid, almost like the frozen lake was trying to take him, too. Max tried to stand, but couldn't. And it was at this moment, the boy lying there on the frozen lake, mouth dripping with blood, that he dimly started to hear the *crunching of boots* in the snow.

Max knew in an instant whose boots they were. He remembered the warning of the shopkeeper as he quietly said to himself, "*Them are Charlie's fish.*"

Max turned to see the bucket strapped to the back of Tyler's snowmobile. The boy rallied every ounce of strength to get back on his feet as the bitter wind and snow relentlessly pounded him.

Max pulled the starter rope on the motorized drill. It roared to life and he set it to the ice, burrowing into the frozen lake. Max leaned his full weight against the drill and—*when it finally broke through*—he fell, losing the drill to frigid lake waters below.

Max dragged himself back to retrieve the bucket of fish. With fingertips that had by now succumbed to frostbite, Max tore the lid of the five-gallon bucket off and towed it back to the hole he had drilled in the ice.

He dumped the fish through the hole and back into the water, then collapsed into a heap. His eyes were frozen shut. He had no feeling in his extremities. Max lay helplessly as the winter storm that would soon take his life howled around him.

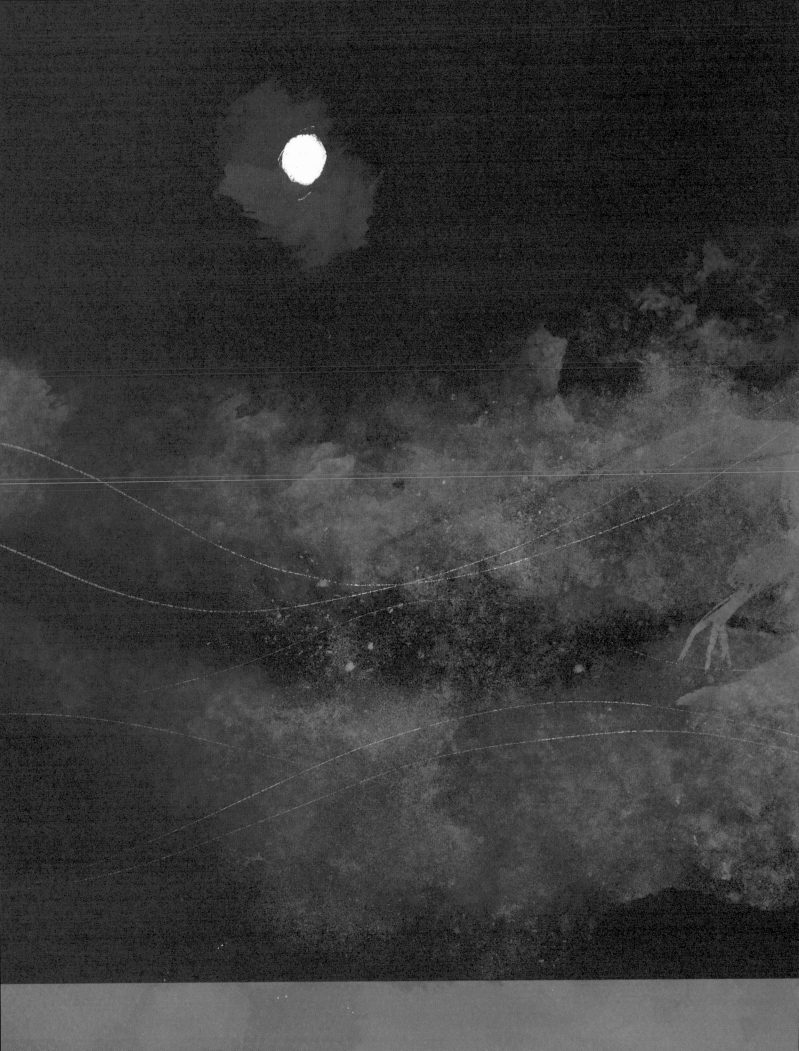

But then—the winds went silent. The bitter cold evaporated. Max flexed his fingers, the feeling slowly coming back to them. He wiped the melting ice from his eyelashes and opened them to see the night was suddenly clear, the full moon illuminating the frozen lake, the road, and the mountain.

A gust of snow rose against the dark, and Max momentarily glimpsed what he swore was the *figure of a man*. A familiar silhouette with piercing eyes staring down at him.

But as soon as the figure had appeared, it was gone, leaving Max alone on the ice surrounding Point Whitney.

fred

Written by Jesse Reffsin
Illustrated by Chris Sasaki

Fred

When hiking, Fred
would always wear
a pack, quite bright and red.

The things he'd stow
would keep him safe,
at least that's what he said.

A knife for bears,
a match for fire,
a lantern for its light.

But the eerie things
that troubled Fred
were those that come at night.

So in Fred's pack
he'd carry things.
Their use I found unclear.

A strange pendant necklace,
a book full of symbols,
an antler from a deer.

It was with that pack
we set out one day
past a river deep and strong.

And after the river
we entered a wood
with trees tall as the river was long.

The trail was well kept,
perfect, in fact,
not a leaf or twig on the ground.

But strangely enough,
though we looked and we looked,
there were no signs of life to be found.

And when I say none,
I really mean none.
Not a footprint. Not a sound.

It wasn't just people,
gone from those woods,
there were also no animals 'round.

This got Fred to thinking,
back then on that trail,
and his voice took an ominous tone:

"An entire forest,
still as the grave,
is better left alone."

Sadly my thoughts
took the opposite tack,
and I pushed us to keep moving on.

The fears gnawing
at Fred's resolve
just served to make mine strong.

But as we moved on,
I did wonder aloud
at the silence that seemed almost dead.

Fred's voice from behind me
sought to give answer
as he clutched at his bag bright and red:

"Woods such as these
are not empty at all.
This one," he said, "feels quite packed—

if you stare off the path
to the crowds of these trees,
it's the trees themselves that stare back."

Poor poor Fred,
I thought, as I saw
how his worries trembled his knees.

He's walking through woods,
on such a fine day,
and all he can see are the trees.

I gave a quick glance,
at the forest around us,
to prove that things were all right.

And that's when I saw,
I'd lost track of the sun.
The day would soon turn to night.

How careless, I thought,
as I looked to my friend,
intending to turn and go home.

59

But to my surprise,
in looking for Fred,
I found that I was alone.

And so I set off
down the way we had come,
thinking that Fred had turned back.

But as darkness rolled
'cross the woods that bleak night,
the path became harder to track.

What had seemed so straight,
so wide, so quick,
now seemed twisted and shrinking

It almost seemed
the path had changed,
a thought I was fearful of thinking.

For what is a path,
when you give the thought pause,
but a space the trees have gifted?

So if you're walking a path,
and you find it has shrunk,
it must be the trees that have shifted.

It was while lost in this thought,
as I wandered the dark,
that I found the first sign of Fred's strife.

Past a bend in the path,
there scattered in dirt:
a lantern, a match, and a knife.

I lit up the lantern,
and used its dim light,
to follow the serpentine trail.

But if ever you've used
a light in the woods,
you know just how it can fail.

For now with my vision
blinded by light,
the forest could do as it pleased.

And that's when it started,
a noise in the woods,
the whisper of leaves in the breeze.

I quickened my pace
as the wind kept on building,
causing bowed branches to groan.

The noise from these woods
howled right through me,
plaintive and deep as a moan.

At this point the trail
had all but closed up,
so I struggled past rough, mossy bark.

I could hardly believe
how right Fred had been
about the things that come out in the dark.

Now, perhaps those woods
had taken offense
to the things Fred had brought in from fear.

For past the next tree
on the ground was a book,
a pendant, an antler of deer.

I grabbed them and ran,
now worried for Fred,
as the mournful wails kept on calling.

I dashed for my life
over branches and roots,
somehow without ever falling.

And at last I came
to the long winding river
that marked the edge of the trees.

So I turned and I looked
at the woods that had held me
perhaps to confirm I was free.

But in turning I saw,
lit by the moon,
a sight that filled me with dread.

High at the top
of an unclimbable tree
was a bag. Quite bright. Quite red.

I stared at that tree
unable to pull
my gaze away from the pack.

And as I stared up
my thoughts were of Fred,
for the tree, indeed, did stare back.

depth

Written by Jesse Reffsin
Illustrated by Jeff Turley

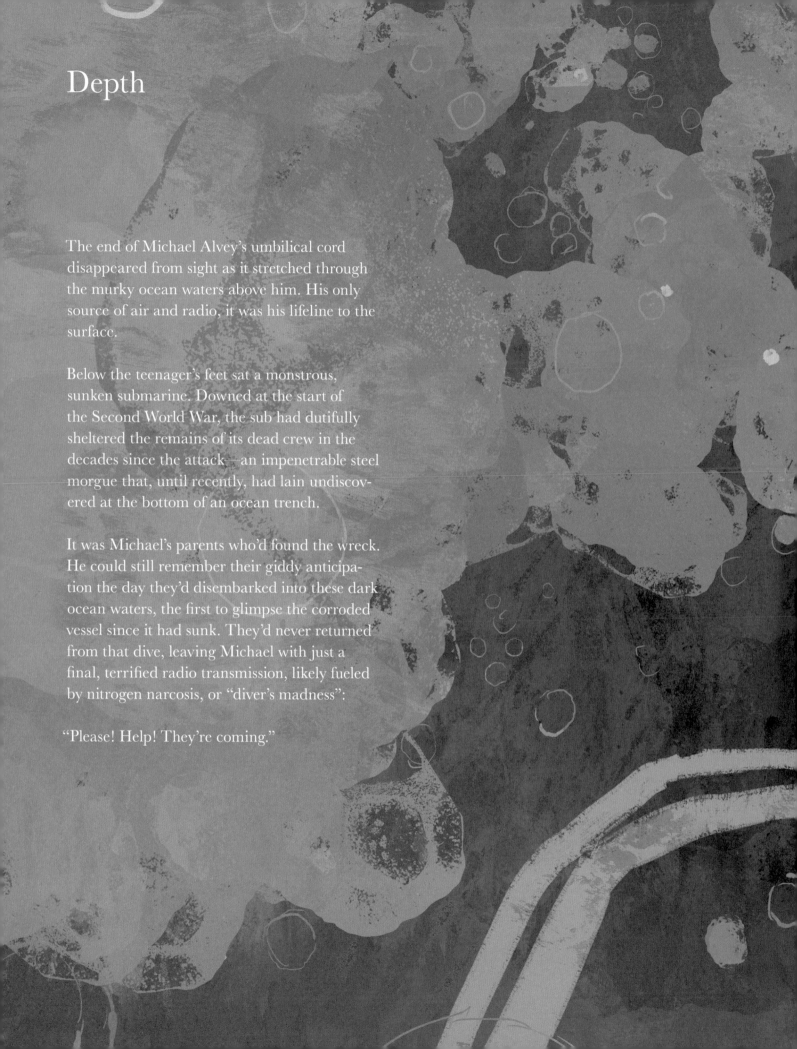

Depth

The end of Michael Alvey's umbilical cord disappeared from sight as it stretched through the murky ocean waters above him. His only source of air and radio, it was his lifeline to the surface.

Below the teenager's feet sat a monstrous, sunken submarine. Downed at the start of the Second World War, the sub had dutifully sheltered the remains of its dead crew in the decades since the attack—an impenetrable steel morgue that, until recently, had lain undiscovered at the bottom of an ocean trench.

It was Michael's parents who'd found the wreck. He could still remember their giddy anticipation the day they'd disembarked into these dark ocean waters, the first to glimpse the corroded vessel since it had sunk. They'd never returned from that dive, leaving Michael with just a final, terrified radio transmission, likely fueled by nitrogen narcosis, or "diver's madness":

"Please! Help! They're coming."

Now it was Michael's duty to retrieve their bodies from the hulking steel beast. Others had offered to spare Michael the sight of his parents' dead bodies, but he knew it had to be him. Last to see them alive, he would be first to see them dead.

Michael moved into action. Clambering across the massive hull of the sub, he arrived at the top hatch. It was sealed shut. His parents must have closed it after entering, locking themselves inside to drown. Michael shuddered at the renewed reminder of their gruesome deaths.

He grabbed the circular wheel that drove the door's latch and strained against its rusty bearings. It groaned with age before finally engaging, freeing the hatch's bolts with a piercing screech. A current of foul water rushed from the opening as Michael pulled the door back to reveal the foreboding interior of the vessel below.

Inside, years of contact with harsh ocean water had bleached the sub bone white. As Michael swam through its dark corridors, a constant haze of algae and bottom-feeders clouded his flashlight's beam. An experienced diver at the age of fifteen, Michael was already accustomed to exploring the wrecks of downed ships. He always found them to have the same

unsettling stillness about them. The stillness of a place familiar with death.

Although a certain doomed malaise was typical on these types of dives, Michael did feel there was something amiss in the vessel. Where were the bodies? Over a hundred sailors had perished on the sub, yet he'd not found a single sign of human remains.

Continuing onward through the haunting quiet of the ship, Michael had more pressing things to worry about than the absent crew. Keeping his umbilical from catching on the turns of the labyrinthine corridors was of chief concern. Even the slightest snag could rupture the line with disastrous results.

Finally, he reached the door at the end of the passage—the engine room. The last room his parents had explored, he knew it was the most likely place to find them.

The ancient door creaked as he pushed it open, his flashlight's beam cutting, almost hesitantly, through the room's dingy water.

There they were. Face down on the floor—his mother and father.

Though Michael had prepared himself for this moment, he found himself overcome with shock. He dropped to his knees, unable to take his eyes off their still forms.

After what seemed an eternity, Michael reached for their faces. He had to see them.

He lifted his father's head first. The sight was
ghastly. The skin hung loose and bloated from his
father's bones, barely recognizable as the man he
had once known. Michael collected his courage and
removed his father's mask. He slowly pried open
his father's eyelids to confirm the diver's madness
that he suspected had taken his life. But Michael
was shocked to find his father's eyes were . . . clear.
There was no sign at all of the redness that was the
telltale sign of narcosis.

His mother's softly rotting eyes showed the same thing. Michael dropped her head and staggered back, unable to believe what he was seeing. If it hadn't been the madness of narcosis that had cost his parents' lives, then what? It didn't make sense.

As Michael reeled in confusion, he felt a sudden tension in his umbilical. Though he'd safeguarded against it, the cord was caught somewhere in the dark maze behind him.

He tugged on the base of the cord, but the snag held strong. He gave another small tug—still nothing. His third pull finally set the cord free. Michael sighed in relief, about to turn back to his parents, when—

THUNK!

Valves automatically slammed shut on Michael's helmet. Water was threatening to force its way inside. It could only mean one thing—the cord had ruptured. Reacting quickly, Michael bit down on his emergency air tube, starting the flow of oxygen from the small tank on his back. The air would last only minutes.

He quickly coiled the umbilical to check the breach. The cord's end only deepened Michael's alarm. It wasn't ruptured at all. It was cut clean through, as if with a knife. Was something out there?

He instinctively turned to his parents for comfort, but found none in the horror stretched across their morbidly distended faces. Their appearances would never again provide the reassurance he had always relied upon.

Michael fled from the haunting sight. He scrambled from the engine room, pushing past the rusted door and into the corridor. Ready to make a dash for it, he suddenly stopped short.

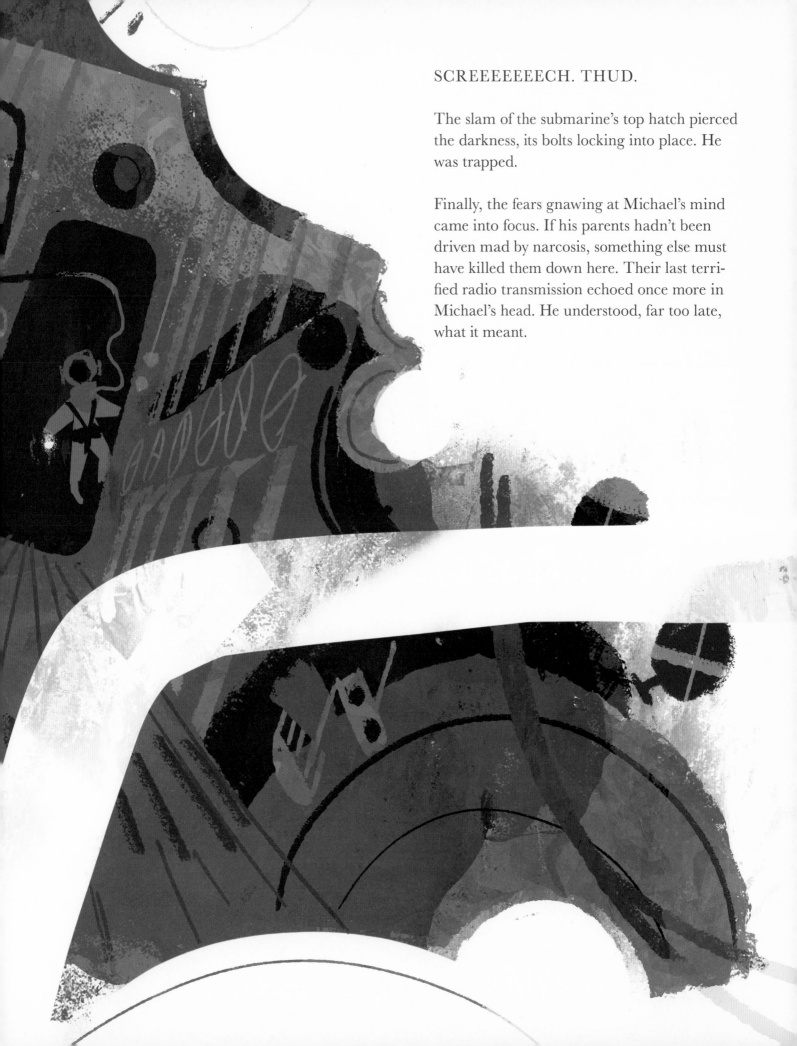

SCREEEEEEECH. THUD.

The slam of the submarine's top hatch pierced the darkness, its bolts locking into place. He was trapped.

Finally, the fears gnawing at Michael's mind came into focus. If his parents hadn't been driven mad by narcosis, something else must have killed them down here. Their last terrified radio transmission echoed once more in Michael's head. He understood, far too late, what it meant.

"Please! Help! They're coming."

Somewhere in the darkness of the sub, another
door groaned open. The ship's crew hadn't been
missing.

They'd been hiding.

the descent

Written by Blaise Hemingway
Illustrated by Chris Sasaki

The Descent

While he waited for the elevator, Christopher looked down at his socks. They were his favorites, long and woolen with rubber grips lining the bottom. On days when he was too sick to go to school, Christopher's mother would retrieve them from his topmost drawer and roll them onto his feet. While the boy had long outgrown the pair, they always brought him comfort.

Christopher's big toe poked out of a hole on the left foot. He rubbed the liberated toe into the rug on which he stood. The coarse wool reminded him of how the nape of his neck felt after a visit to the barber.

PING!

The elevator doors rumbled open. The car was empty, which was no real surprise considering the late hour. *What time is it?* thought Christopher. *Past midnight, I'm sure.*

As Christopher stepped inside, the car creaked under his weight, which—him being of below-average weight and height for an 11-year-old—was slightly unnerving.

The elevator looked very old, certainly much older than his parents and likely older than his grandparents. Christopher ran his fingertips along the hand-carved wooden paneling lining

the elevator's interior. He could tell it was real wood, unlike the vinyl laminate on the inside of the elevator at the medical building.

The boy turned to his right to make his selection from the car's numbered buttons, only to find: *no buttons*. He turned left and saw none there either. *Odd*, thought Christopher. The boy spun, searching the entire elevator for the numbered buttons, to no avail.

PING!

Christopher craned back around quickly, just in time to see the doors close. The boy cursed under his breath. How was he supposed to get anywhere without any buttons?

He tried to relax. Perhaps this was an express elevator, and hence, no buttons were necessary. Christopher waited for something to happen, but the elevator car remained perfectly still.

Despite his best efforts not to, Christopher started to become uneasy. The boy had never really considered himself a claustrophobic person, but he'd also never been inside an unmoving, buttonless elevator car in the middle of the night. Christopher started chewing his thumbnail, a habit his mother detested but that he reserved the right to do in situations like these.

The antique elevator car suddenly lurched downward. Caught off guard, Christopher stumbled sideways and into the wooden panels of the car, which cracked slightly from the impact.

Christopher heard the low and steady hum of a motor. He was still moving. He sighed in relief, but was surprised that—when he did—he could see his own breath. Christopher felt a sudden chill; his hands went to his bare arms to rub his goose-bumped skin, attempting to warm himself.

The light inside the elevator began to flicker. Christopher looked to the ceiling and noticed that one of the two bulbs lighting the car was failing. He could hear the buzzing of the bulb's filament. He remembered his grandfather calling that buzzing "the swan song," the sound you hear right before the bulb goes out. Christopher hoped this swan song would last at least as long as the ride.

The car jerked to a stop, and the doors opened. There, standing in silhouette, was a very old man with white hair combed over his scalp. He was dressed sharply in a green corduroy suit and bow tie with a white pocket square.

"Eve'nin'," said the old man as he stepped onto the elevator. The boy smiled politely but said nothing back. The old man noticed a piece of lint on his jacket sleeve. He carefully pinched it in between his thumb and index fingers, removed it, and dropped it to the floor. "Got married in this suit and it still fits," said the man proudly.

Despite the old man's pleasant demeanor, there was something *off* about him—his skin looked like it was caked with that thick, skin-colored makeup that his mother wore when she had an unsightly blemish to conceal.

PING!

The doors closed, and the elevator resumed its descent. Christopher noticed the old man looked as confused as Christopher felt as he searched about the elevator car's interior. The boy mustered up the courage to say, "There's no buttons," his nervous voice cracking a little. "What floor were you going to?" The old man turned to Christopher and then raised his hand to his head, scratching his comb-over to reveal a large liver spot.

PING!

"I . . . I don't remember," said the old man.

"Oh," said the boy, only now realizing that he could neither recall which floor he wanted to go to nor why he was on this elevator to begin with.

It was then that the car's blinking light bulb blew out, its smoldering filament clouding the bulb with smoke. Christopher nervously turned to check on the only other remaining light bulb, which—for the time being—was still in working order.

PING!

The doors closed, and the woman turned her back to them, revealing what looked like the skid marks of a car tire on her blouse. Christopher turned to the old man, trying to draw his attention to the markings on the woman's blouse, but the old man was in his own world, trying to remember what he was doing there.

As the elevator continued its descent, the boy noticed a crimson-colored puddle next to the woman's broken heel. A steady flow of droplets plopped into the puddle, splashing onto the woman's shoes and stockings. Christopher's eyes followed the droplets back to the source, seeing that they were coming from the woman's fingertips, which were covered in blood.

Christopher gasped with concern. "Ma'am. *Your hand*. It's bleeding." The woman—who still seemed in a haze—eerily lifted her bleeding hand in front of her face and stared at it, unfazed.

The old man immediately drew the white pocket square from his jacket and wrapped it around the woman's hand. The woman didn't protest, but remained silent as the old man went to work to try to stop the bleeding. It wasn't long before the pocket square was saturated with blood.

The elevator again stopped abruptly, and its doors rattled open. Christopher turned to see—this time—a woman, no more than forty years old, stepping on, wearing a white blouse and skirt, her hair slightly askew. She walked awkwardly, which the boy quickly surmised was due to the fact that one of her shoes was missing its heel. The woman teeter-tottered into the car, greeting neither the boy nor the old man.

PING!

The remaining bulb lighting the elevator started to buzz, its filament blinking. Christopher eyed it nervously as he heard the woman's hollow voice for the first time: "Why bother?" She stared defiantly at the old man, who was still actively trying to stop the bleeding.

"Because . . . you're hurt," said the old man. "You're bleeding . . . *badly*." Christopher looked at the floor of the elevator, which was now vanishing beneath the pool of the woman's blood. Christopher backed away into the corner of the elevator, trying to escape it, but his socks were already absorbing blood like a sponge.

The woman shook her head, laughing at the old man. "Don't be a fool." The old man looked back at the woman, puzzled. Christopher, now more terrified than ever, could barely hear their exchange over the high-pitched shriek of the elevator's engine as it began to accelerate.

Tears rolled down Christopher's face. Fear overcame him as he shouted, "I wanna go home. I wanna go home!"

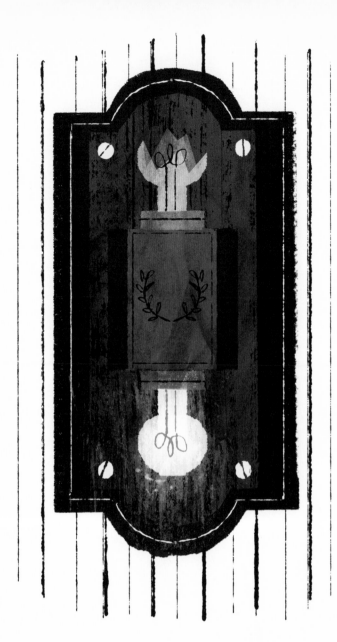

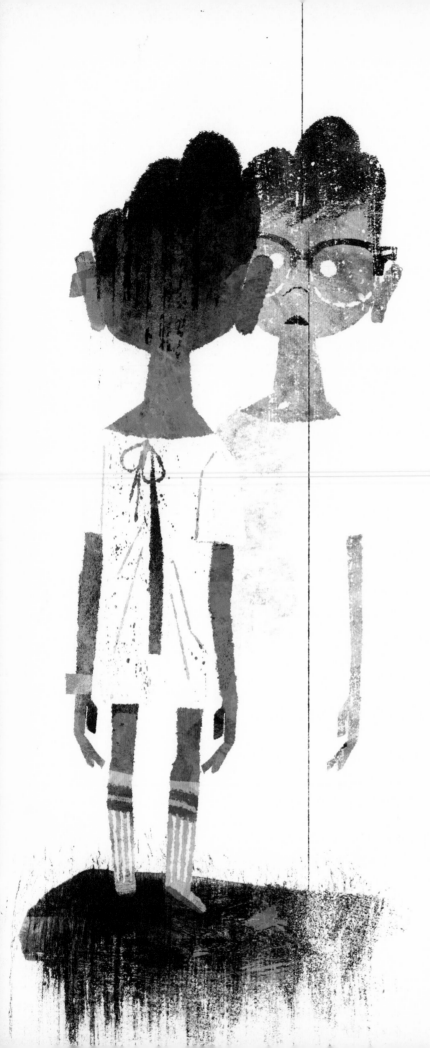

The lone bulb flickered furiously, creating a strobe effect inside the elevator car as the woman turned to Christopher. "You're not going home. *None of us are.*" The woman stepped away from the polished brass elevator doors allowing Christopher to catch a glimpse of his own reflection. The boy saw that he was dressed only in a hospital gown.

"I don't . . . I don't understand . . ."

The old man put his hand over his mouth as he softly uttered, "*Oh no.*"

Christopher looked to the old man. "What? What is it?"

The old man just shook his head, repeating, "I'm so sorry, son. I'm so sorry."

The sound of the elevator's engine was now deafening. Christopher clung to the old man, screaming at the top of his lungs, "*What's happening!?!*" But when the old man finally spoke, the boy couldn't hear a word. Christopher narrowed his eyes, focusing on the old man's lips, trying to read the words he was repeating over and over and *over.*

Christopher slowly deciphered the old man's words, one at time, until he knew them all. As the last bulb blew out, swallowing the car in total darkness, the boy formed the words himself.

"We are all dead."

PING!

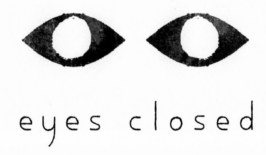

eyes closed

Written by Blaise Hemingway
Illustrated by Chris Sasaki

Eyes Closed

"Keep your eyes closed," said Grace softly to herself. The girl lay awake with the covers pulled up over her head, her nervous breaths making the air hot and stale.

Grace was afraid. The creaking inside her bedroom was getting increasingly louder and she didn't dare make eye contact with the ghost that was responsible for it.

Grace—like all children—knew that so long as you never looked at a ghost, it could do you no harm. Even beneath the sheets and heavy blankets, the girl kept her eyes shut firmly to ensure she didn't accidentally glimpse it.

THUD. Grace shuddered. Was that her bedroom door slamming closed? Or had the ghost knocked something off her dresser to tempt her to look?

Grace quieted her breathing and listened carefully. She could hear the dull whistle of a swirling wind encircling her bed, and she knew . . . the ghost was closer.

The noises started the night Grace moved from the room she shared with her younger sister into this new one. The move came at Grace's own insistence; *after all*, she was ten years old, far too mature to be sharing a room with Molly, a mere first grader who thought only of first-grader things. But now—with terrifying noises inundating her room every night—Grace knew that she had made a terrible mistake. Never once had the ghost come to the bedroom she shared with Molly. Never once did Grace need to hide beneath her blankets. Never once had she lain awake with her eyes closed tightly in fear—

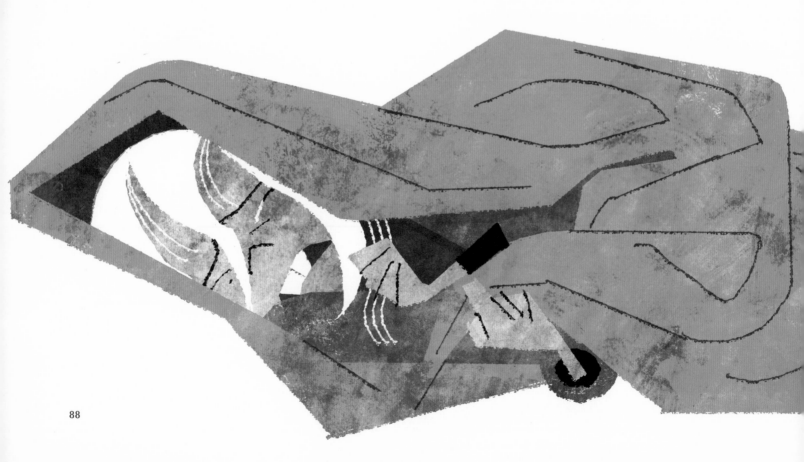

Grace felt something breathing on her toes. *A cold breath.* She quickly drew her feet beneath the covers and pulled her knees into her chest. How a quilted comforter protected her from the ghost remained a mystery, but she nevertheless felt much safer beneath it.

"Keep your eyes closed," Grace repeated.

Grace couldn't tell her parents she wanted to go back, not after relentlessly bugging them about getting her own room. There were no indications that Molly was having any problems since Grace's departure. In fact, Molly seemed perfectly content to be rid of her older sister. How immature would Grace look if *she* was the one too scared to sleep alone and not her younger sibling?

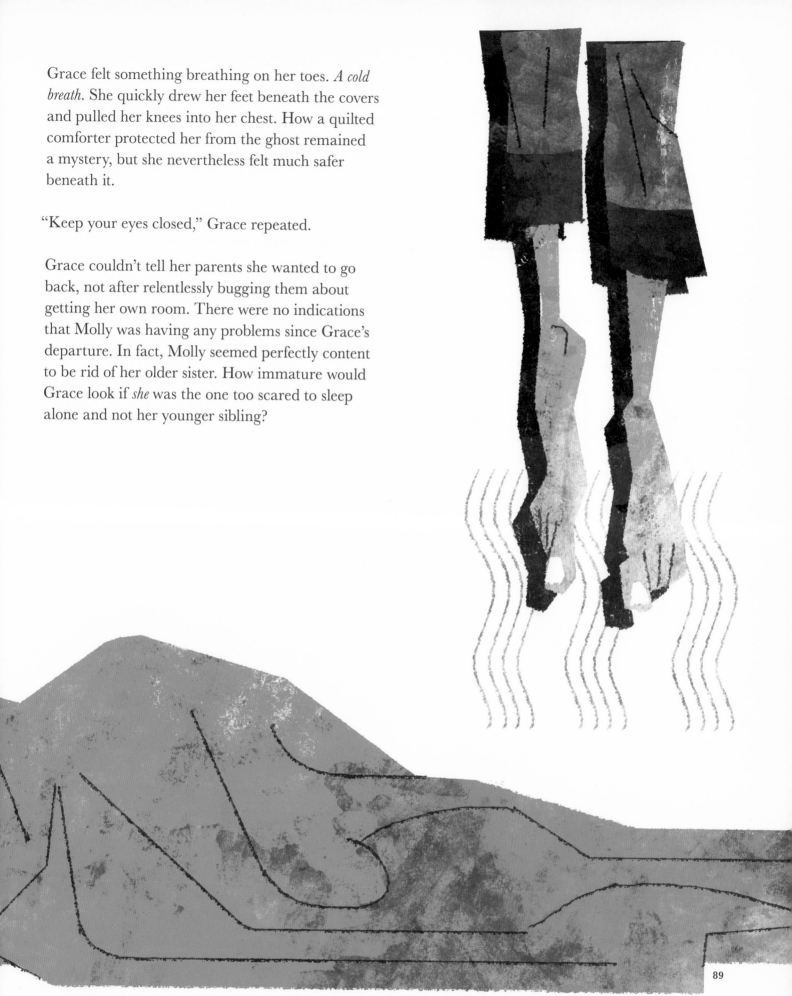

Grace could now hear the scrape of fingernails against the walls of her room. Deliberate and sustained, the nails slowly clawed from her doorway, past her dresser, and over her head as they made their way around the room. The noise paused.

Grace felt her pulse quicken; her heart beat with such intensity that her nightgown bounced up and down against her chest. She knew the ghost was close to her now, probably hovering just above her bed.

Grace pressed her eyelids together as hard as she could. She felt the tension in every muscle on her face; it was painful, but necessary to ensure her protection.

"Keep your eyes closed," Grace said once more, as if a mantra to keep her safe.

The fear was consuming Grace. It had never been this bad before. She considered screaming; the ghost would most certainly vanish once her mother and father rushed into the room. Grace could tell them that it was just a nightmare. They wouldn't have to know the truth. She could preserve her dignity. *But then what?* Grace's parents would return to bed, and soon after, the haunting would resume, perhaps even worse than before. *No.* That wouldn't do.

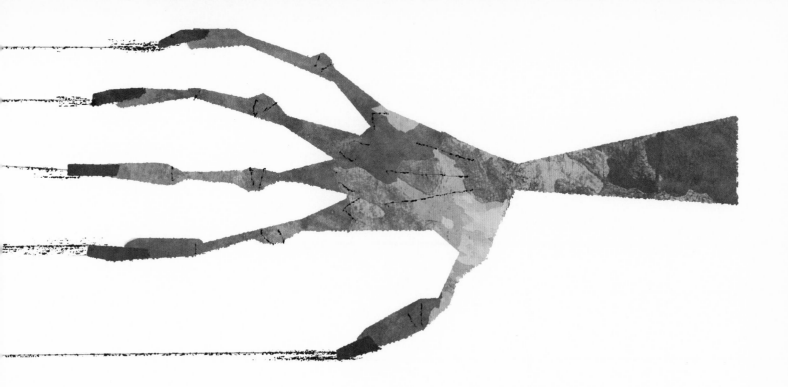

It was then that a thought began to form in Grace's head. A new thought. A bold thought. A liberating thought . . .

Perhaps there was no ghost.

The sounds Grace heard *were* strange, but—*then again*—it wasn't unusual for a house to creak in winter, *especially* an older house like this one. Perhaps Grace never heard the creaking before because it was impossible to hear *anything* over the obnoxious sound of Molly grinding her teeth in her sleep.

The cold breath she'd felt on her toes was probably nothing more than a draft coming from her window. Perhaps it was just slightly ajar and needed to be closed. That would also explain the dull whistle she'd heard.

And as for the clawing, Grace guessed that it was a mouse trapped in the insulation behind the plaster. Mice were known to burrow inside walls to make their nests. A scurrying mouse was the only logical explanation for what she thought were fingernails dragging against the wall.

Furthermore, Grace had never seen the ghost. *Not once.* Granted, she'd never opened her eyes, but . . . wasn't it possible that by not opening her eyes, her imagination had gotten the best of her?

Grace felt foolish. This was all absurd. There was no ghost. She'd imagined the whole thing. Of course she had. How childish of her. She was a ten-year-old girl who—in just a few months— would be attending middle school. Grace was practically a teenager; she had no time to play these silly games. Besides, it was so miserable beneath these blankets, clammy and suffocating.

Enough was enough.

Grace tossed back the comforters, taking a deep breath and feeling the fresh air on her face. The tension melted away. Grace shook her head, wondering why she'd put herself through all that stress for nothing.

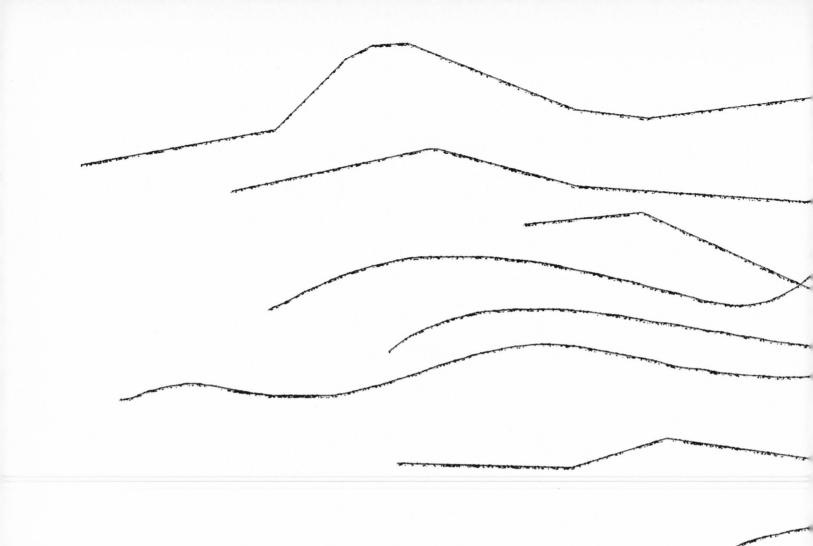

Grace rubbed her eyes and finally opened them. Slowly, the room came into focus, until at last she could clearly see a milky, shifting shape floating over her bed.

The apparition smiled.

"You should have kept your eyes closed."

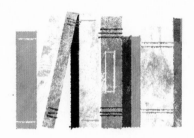

the library

Written by Jesse Reffsin
Illustrated by Jeff Turley

The Library

Meg Harvin had never been to the library; not
many people went these days. But her teacher
had given the class the assignment to check out
a book—an actual book, he had stressed. Paper,
not zeros and ones. So here Meg was, at the front
desk, waiting for help from the librarian.

She had heard about the old woman—everyone
had. The children of the town did their best to
stay clear of her, as they often did with people
they found a bit . . . off.

The woman had been in charge of the town
library for as long as anyone could remember.
That was saying a lot, considering the building
was almost as old as the town itself. Of course,
nobody would suggest that she had been its
librarian the entire time. But no one could imag-
ine the library without the old woman, who was
most often seen walking among the dusty shelves,
tending the books. Meg had heard that she cared
for them as if they were her own children.

"Let me guess, Mr. Morrissey's class?" The
librarian shuffled out from behind a stack, giving
Meg a start.

"Uh, yeah. I'm looking for—"

"A book." The woman winked. "I know, been a
whole rash of you, just lookin' for books. Follow
me."

She turned and pushed deeper into the library's recesses. Meg gave a glance around the old building. It wasn't the most inviting place. Large and cavernous, it easily let in the drafty winter air from outside. The chill seemed undaunted by the fire that crackled in the large stone hearth. The space had been used for barracks during the Revolutionary War. It seemed to have kept the foreboding of a place intended to house those not long for this world.

"You coming?"

Meg looked up to find the woman staring at her from the steps that led to the library's lower level. Before Meg could answer, the librarian descended into the building's depths, her heels clicking on the worn stairs. Meg wondered why they couldn't just stick with the books on the main level. She sighed as she hurried to follow the woman down.

The bottom level of the library was somehow even draftier than above, which Meg found puzzling since they were now underground. Green-shaded lamps lit the winding stacks of books, but Meg couldn't help feeling that the space would have been more at home in the flicker of dying candlelight.

"I call this the tomb," the librarian cut into her thoughts.

Meg looked up, nervously. "You do?"

The librarian grinned and shook her head. "No. I call it nonfiction."

Meg smiled; the woman had picked up on her unease. Meg guessed it was kind of silly to be put off by a building. "Sorry, my first time here. I wasn't expecting it to be so . . ."

"Old?"

Meg nodded, apologetically. The librarian smiled. "You're a good one. I can tell. Lots of Morrissey's kids come through here, and they're not so nice. They don't respect things that are old."

She turned to continue on through the shelves. Meg noticed, curiously, that the woman had a habit of reaching out to pat the books as she passed. It seemed she was very deliberate about the ones she touched—only those that protruded from the shelf, that were for some reason pushed forward. From the way they stuck out past the other books, it almost looked as if they were trying to escape.

"Some of the children that show up act as though I'm burdening them. As if being around books takes a toll. Do you believe that, sweetie?"

Meg was still thinking about the woman's odd habit of singling out books as she walked by. The whispers she'd heard seemed true— the way the old woman patted those books, it was as if she was comforting a child.

Meg looked up to find the woman staring at her, waiting for a response.

"Sorry?" Meg hazarded, not realizing she had been asked a question.

"Are you one of those children that doesn't like to spend time around books?" The librarian began cracking her knuckles, ominously, as she waited for a response.

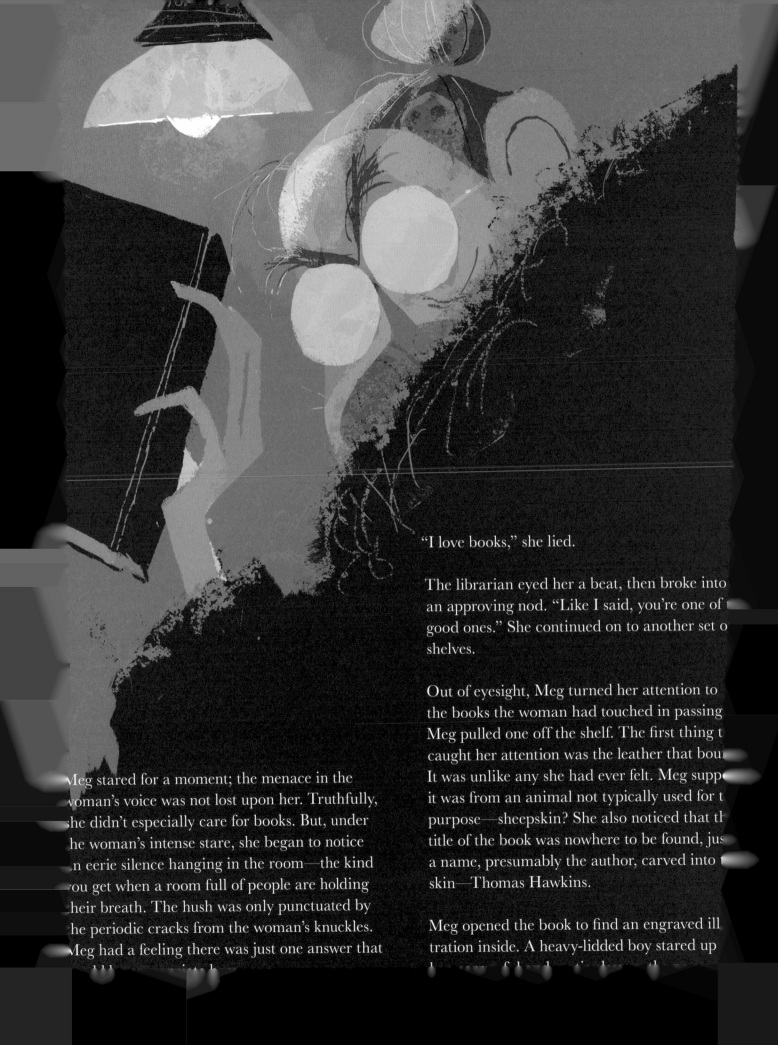

"I love books," she lied.

The librarian eyed her a beat, then broke into an approving nod. "Like I said, you're one of good ones." She continued on to another set o shelves.

Out of eyesight, Meg turned her attention to the books the woman had touched in passing Meg pulled one off the shelf. The first thing t caught her attention was the leather that bou It was unlike any she had ever felt. Meg supp it was from an animal not typically used for t purpose—sheepskin? She also noticed that th title of the book was nowhere to be found, jus a name, presumably the author, carved into skin—Thomas Hawkins.

Meg opened the book to find an engraved ill tration inside. A heavy-lidded boy stared up

Meg stared for a moment; the menace in the woman's voice was not lost upon her. Truthfully, she didn't especially care for books. But, under the woman's intense stare, she began to notice an eerie silence hanging in the room—the kind you get when a room full of people are holding their breath. The hush was only punctuated by the periodic cracks from the woman's knuckles. Meg had a feeling there was just one answer that

"Ah. Thomas." Meg looked up at the sound of the librarian's voice. She was standing beside her, staring at the illustration. After taking a moment to eye the thin black lines that comprised the boy, the woman smiled and pulled the book from Meg's hand.

"You know what I've found? When children spend enough time around books, even the worst ones seem to come around. In the end." With that, she closed the cover on the illustrated boy, whose eyes seemed still to stare out at Meg as the pages shut over him. The librarian put him back on the shelf.

"Now follow me. That particular book isn't for you." The woman pushed on as Meg gave a backward glance toward the shelf she was leaving behind. She noticed that all the books the librarian had touched were bound in that same, odd leather.

As she turned to follow the woman, she couldn't help thinking back to the boy's pleading eyes as he was shut into darkness, trapped between the pages of the book.

"Here you go, dear." The librarian had stopped at another shelf. "Architecture. Figured you might be interested to learn a little more about old buildings, like this one?"

Meg nodded. She was now firmly of the opinion that she didn't want to contradict the woman, even though a book about old architecture sounded frightfully boring.

The woman smiled in satisfaction. She clapped her hands together. "I knew it!" She handed a book over to Meg and led the way back toward the stairs, still unconsciously grazing her hands against the spines of the books that jutted past their neighbors. Meg couldn't shake the feeling, even stronger now, that the books were straining to free themselves from the shelves that held them.

Meg looked the books over as she followed the woman. Each read the same—no title, just a name cut deep into the odd leather. Book after book, name after name.

Finally, her curiosity got the best of her and she pulled another one of the heavy tomes down. She opened the book to find an illustration of a wisp of a girl. The girl had dark shadows under her eyes, and she almost appeared to be wailing as she stared out from her page. Meg stared back for a moment, before closing the cover and putting the girl back on the shelf with just a tinge of fright.

She walked farther and pulled another book down. A second girl peered out; tears had traced streaks down her face. In another book, Meg could only see the back of a boy—he faced away, as if made to stare at a wall in punishment. Another book held a boy curled into a terrified ball in the corner of the page. Each book she opened contained another child in despair.

Finally she came to the last book on the shelf. She stopped, in surprise. It bore her own name—Meg Harvin. As she eyed the book, apprehensively, the librarian's voice floated back in from the stairs.

"Meg, you are telling me the truth, yes? You truly do love books?"

Meg looked up, taken aback that the woman knew her name. She forced out a weak response. "Of course."

The woman nodded, solemnly.

"Then there's no need for you to open that book. Come upstairs. We'll get you checked out."

The woman disappeared, her heels clicking once more on the old stone steps. Meg turned to take a last look at the book that bore her name. She shivered in the chill air that gusted through the stacks. Finally, she turned and followed the librarian, leaving the book unopened.

Behind her, there was the faintest rustle of pages, and then silence.

the boy in
the basement

Written by Jesse Reffsin
Illustrated by Chris Sasaki

The Boy in
the Basement

"Welcome home!"

Ellie Stenson stared in shock as her dad yelled
over the car engine. She stayed in the passenger
seat, watching him turn off the car and walk
up the stoop of their new house. She turned
to their Great Dane, Kellogg. "He can't be
serious. Can he?"

She couldn't understand how her dad could
want to live in such a place. Setting aside that
they were practically in the middle of nowhere,
this house was a wreck. Actually, it was down-
right scary. The structure loomed overhead,
almost villainously. Ivy cut across its façade
like a deep scar.

"Ellie, come on! Don't you wanna see?"
He ducked inside the foyer. Ellie
sighed and trudged up the steps,
Kellogg sniffing skeptically at
the air. Maybe it was nice
on the inside?

Nope, not even close. The place looked like it hadn't been cleaned in ages. Layers of dust and cobwebs covered every surface, and the stench of mildew filled the rooms. Ellie turned away so her dad wouldn't catch her disappointment.

That's when she saw it—the door off the kitchen. Somehow, it looked even older than the rest of the house. Its aged and grooved wood made it seem as though the house had been built around it. There was also a latch. It was padlocked shut.

"Oh, come on!" her dad called out, disappointed. "They said they'd take the lock off before they left." He had come up behind her as she was staring at the door. Ellie had to admit, from the look of it, she was happy it was locked.

"What is it?" she asked, doing her best to conceal her unease.

"Basement," he replied offhandedly as he turned to go back outside.

"Where are you going?"

He looked at her with a mischievous smile. "My tools are in the car. Gonna have to break that lock off."

When he came back, a hammer hung loosely from his hand. He pulled a flashlight from his pocket and set it on the table, then Ellie watched as he lined the hammer up with the padlock. Her apprehension built as he brought it back, ready to crack the lock in two. WHACK!

The lock crumbled and fell from the latch. It must have been nearly as old as the door itself. Her dad pulled the heavy wood back, exposing . . .

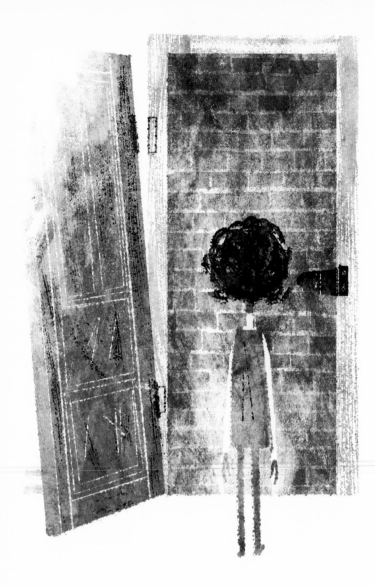

Ellie's dreams brought no rest from the new surroundings. In her sleep, she drifted back to the kitchen, slowly crossing the old wooden floor, drawn to the mysterious door. She turned the creaky handle to find the brick was now gone. In its place was a set of stairs twisting their way into the pitch-black basement below.

As she stared, a gust of rancid air floated out of the darkness. It was followed by a ragged voice:

"NO KIDS ALLOWED UPSTAIRS."

Ellie gasped as she woke with a start, her heart pounding. She tried to control her breathing and shake off the bad dream. She was relieved when she looked up to find Kellogg walking into her room. He must have heard her restless sleep. His presence calmed her, and they both slept through the rest of the night.

The next day Ellie found herself in front of the basement door. Of course she knew it had just been a dream. But still, she had to check. She cautiously opened the old wooden door. Behind it she found bricks. Nothing more. She felt stupid for even looking. What did she expect to find?

"I called the previous owners this morning." Ellie turned to find her dad walking into the kitchen. "Said it'd been like that since before they bought the place. Used to be someone's room, but for some reason it was bricked up."

A wall. The opening had been bricked over. The basement was permanently blocked off.

"Are you kidding me?" Ellie's dad exclaimed in frustration.

Ellie gave the bricks a worried glance. The old door, the lock, the walled-up entrance—why were they there? To keep people from going down? Or was it the other way around?

That night, Ellie's new mattress was laid out on the creaky floorboards of her room. Her dad said they'd be able to put her bed frame together the next day. For now her room was just essentials. It didn't really feel like she lived there.

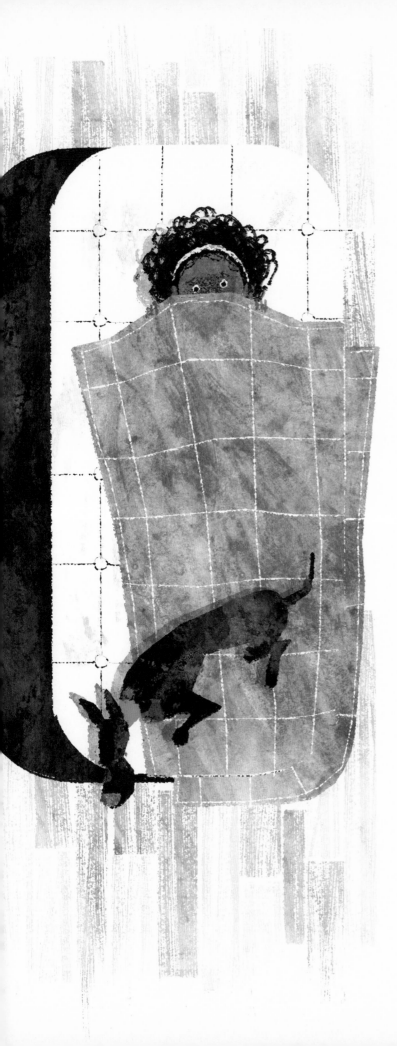

Ellie turned back to the wall in horror. "Someone lived down there?"

"I guess." Her dad shrugged, walking up from behind. "Just bugs me we can't get into our own basement."

Ellie's eyes widened. She turned to her dad. "Dad, you're not gonna take it down, are you?!" she asked, pleadingly. She hadn't realized it until then, but a sick sense of dread had been building in her the more she thought about the basement.

Her dad, seeing the terror on his daughter's face, knelt down, kindly. "El, don't worry. I couldn't even if I wanted to." He gave the bricks a hard SLAP. "Old house like this has settled by now. It's load bearing. We take this away, the roof's liable to come down on us."

Ellie gave a nod, relieved. She was surer than ever that she never wanted to find out what was down there.

That night, Ellie slept with Kellogg in her bed once again. Her room was starting to come together. Her dad had built her bed frame and had even brought in a nightstand and dresser for her. But no matter how cozy they made the room, she didn't feel comfortable there.

Still, with her dog by her side, she was eventually able to drift off to sleep. Though her dreams brought her right back to the basement door. This time, as she got closer, she began to hear an insistent scratching from the other side. Something was down there, and it wanted out.

Even knowing it was just a dream, this was too much for her. She turned to go before . . . WHOOSH! The door flew open of its own accord.

Once more, the bricks were gone. The darkness beyond them was solid. Ellie backed away, frightened. Even though she felt a strange pull toward the door, she knew not to go past it. It seemed it had no power to make her cross the basement's threshold.

As she backed away, she caught sight of something that deepened her fear. She hoped it was just her mind playing tricks on her, but something appeared to be moving in the darkness below.

"Hello?" she called out cautiously. "Who's down there?"

The only response was muffled steps as someone began to climb the old stairs. Whatever was down there, it was coming up. She tried to shuffle away, but her frantic movement only caused her to trip.

As she lay on the creaky floor, she waited in horror for what she might see at the top of the stairs. But whatever it was, it never showed itself, stopping midway up the steps. The only thing that came through the doorway was the sound of the voice, again carried by the dank, dead air.

"NO KIDS ALLOWED UPSTAIRS."

Once again, she woke with a fright, the voice echoing fearfully in her head. She shuddered to think of what it could mean, turning to her dog for comfort. Except he was nowhere to be seen.

"Kellogg!" She searched all over her room, thinking that maybe he had just hopped down to the floor. It wasn't until she had thoroughly searched that she began to hear the faint barking. He was downstairs.

Following his barks down to the kitchen, she found that she could hear them, faintly . . . coming from the other side of the basement door. "Not possible," she said to herself. But still, she had to make sure. She reached out and opened the door, fearful of what she'd find.

The brick wall was gone. She shook her head. This couldn't be happening. She pinched herself to make sure it wasn't a dream. It wasn't.

She reached for the light switch. It was dead. She grabbed the flashlight, still lying on the kitchen table from when her dad put it there.

Dad! The thought hit her. Should she warn him she was going down there? Another insistent round of barks filtered up from the basement. She didn't have time to waste. Kellogg was in trouble. She clicked on the beam of her flashlight—it barely helped to pierce the darkness below.

She made her way down the twisting staircase. It creaked with neglect as she pushed onward. The smell at the bottom was the first thing to hit her. Ten times worse than the gusts that had floated up in her dreams. Most basements are musty and dank, but this place had something else. Something dead.

She stooped to walk through the cramped space. Navigating with the flashlight proved futile, its dim beam barely able to make out rough shapes along the floor. What those shapes were was anyone's guess. At one point, her foot grazed something that felt almost—soft. She shined her light at it. She felt crazy for thinking it, but from what she could make out in the darkness, the shape looked a bit human. Spindly limbs, wildly matted hair, and the smell . . . the smell was even worse here.

She stepped away from the indistinct form with a shudder. She couldn't help but think back to what her dad had said, how this place had once been someone's room. The thought was too much. She had to get out.

Suddenly, she heard Kellogg's bark, but this time, it was not coming from the basement at all. It was coming from the top of the stairs. She looked back across the basement to the steps; light from the kitchen seeped down to the bottom. She could see her dog's shadow cast against it.

"Kellogg!" She ran back to the stairs. She got to the bottom and looked up. Kellogg was staring down at her, worried and whimpering. She had one long, last look at him before . . . SLAM. The door swung shut.

"No!" She ran up the stairs, but she already knew what she would find at the top. Bricks, mortar—a wall. She was trapped.

"Help! HELP!"

She could hear her dog barking like mad from the other side of the door. The sound of his frantic scratching carried through both the door and the brick wall to her. Finally, she heard her dad walk into the kitchen.

"Kellogg! What are you doing?! Look at what you've done to this door. Out! Right this instant!"

"No! Dad! Help! I'm trapped!"

There was a pause from the other side of the door. Finally, she heard her dad once more. "I said out!"

He couldn't hear her.

As Ellie listened to her dad's footsteps recede through the kitchen, she sat down on the top step of the dark basement. There was no way out.

As this thought finally hit her, she heard a creak from the bottom of the stairs.

She turned the ever-dimming flashlight. Staring up at her, with its matted hair, spindly limbs, and torn clothing, was the shape from the floor. Ellie stared in fright for a moment, before the thing smiled sickly. Its cracked and hideous lips exposed a mouth of decaying teeth.

It was the last thing she saw as the flashlight finally gave out, plunging her into darkness. The ragged voice floated up to her from the bottom of the stairs, one more time.

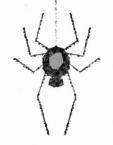

widow
in black

Written by Jesse Reffsin
Illustrated by Jeff Turley

Widow in Black

The children surrounded the spider on the splintered platform of the old wooden play structure. It was a game they often played, rooting spiders out of hiding and chasing them through the playground. These types of spiders were common in the crevices of the weathered wood—big but not dangerous. Most spiders aren't—dangerous, that is—but they can get quite large all the same.

This spider was scrambling back and forth inside the circle of children. Each time it seemed it would get away, a child would bring its foot down with a loud THUMP, driving the spider back toward the middle. Finally the leader of the group, a particularly ugly boy, brought his boot down on the spider. CRUNCH. The children laughed as he wiped guts onto the edge of the play structure, then kicked what was left of the spider's body onto the mulch below. The children went off in search of another, so wrapped up in their fun that they failed to notice . . .

. . . the old widow on the edge of the playground. Her heavy clothes were out of place for the hot summer day, especially her sweater—a lumpy cocoon of black wool. In fact her clothes hung so heavy, dark, and loose that they had the effect of making the old woman seem almost formless, merely a dark shape. She hunched over a shopping cart bundled with old clothes, shuffling her feet as she followed the sidewalk that circled the playground. Her eyes were fixed on the children.

THUMP!

The children had chased another spider out of hiding, this one larger than the last. They giggled as they watched it dart across the wood, its panic evident in its swift movements.

"You're being cruel, you know." The children turned at the sound of the widow's voice, taking their first notice of her. The spider seized the opportunity to skitter away, finding refuge in a new section of the wooden play structure.

"Great. You let it get away!" the ugly boy yelled at the widow. She just nodded, satisfied, and continued pushing her cart along the sidewalk. The boy rolled his eyes as he turned back to the group. "Creepy old lady," he said, dismissively. The children murmured their agreement, turning to search for another spider.

None of the children looked at the widow long enough to spot the thread trailing from her sweater. It had snagged on a tree branch, but she didn't seem to notice, quietly pushing her cart along the sidewalk as she continued to circle the children.

It didn't take long for the children to find a new spider, but this one they didn't scare out of hiding right away. It was feeding—something the children rarely got to see, but which interested them to no end.

They watched as a fly, trapped in the spider's web, frantically thrashed against the silk that held it prisoner. It was no use, of course. The web would not break; it was made of a material far stronger than the fly. The only thing the fly did accomplish was to alert the spider to its presence, its struggles vibrating along the strands of web. The spider clambered to its captive as the children watched, transfixed.

As the fly gave a last fruitless effort to free itself, the hungry predator unsheathed a gigantic pair of fangs and plunged them deep into its prey's exoskeleton. The fly writhed in pain as venom pumped into its body. The toxins worked fast, using the fly's circulatory system against it. When the spider withdrew its meaty fangs the poison had already begun its work, paralyzing the fly.

While the children watched the morbid scene with glee, the widow continued to shuffle around the playground. Had there been any bystanders, they might have alerted the old woman to her fast-unraveling sweater. They also might have noticed that, with so much thread lost, the sweater was giving way to a hint of slick, jet-black skin underneath.

Meanwhile, the ugly boy watched with fascination as the spider wrapped the fly in a sticky sack of webbing, using its many legs to rotate its prey in silk spun from its abdomen. The fly lay immobile, helpless to fight against its inevitable end.

The tiny insect could see the children through the light layer of webbing over its eyes. Of course, to the fly they were nothing more than gigantic figures against the fast-disappearing sky. If it could recognize them as creatures at all, the fly would have been disheartened by the grins stretched across their faces and the apparent joy they were drawing from its last moments alive. They could easily have saved the fly, but the thought never even entered their minds.

As she went on walking the perimeter, thread from the widow's sweater now surrounded the playground many times over. The sweater itself was almost gone, and the widow looked increasingly more disquieting. Her skin shone in the sun, as if covered in gloss. Short, thick hairs standing straight out of her back bristled in the wind. Gigantic masses protruded from her side, eight in all, black as the rest of her once-concealed body and folded around her tightly.

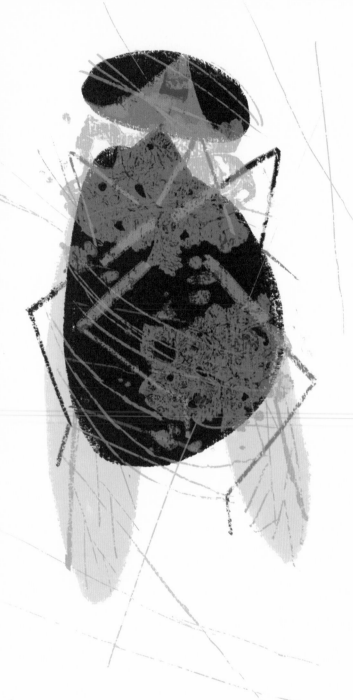

CRUNCH!

The ugly boy lifted his boot. He had gotten both the spider and the fly in one swift motion. "Two for one." He grinned as he wiped guts off the sole of his shoe. The spider's web clung to his shoe as well, its sticky residue still doing its job. The boy didn't bother removing it.

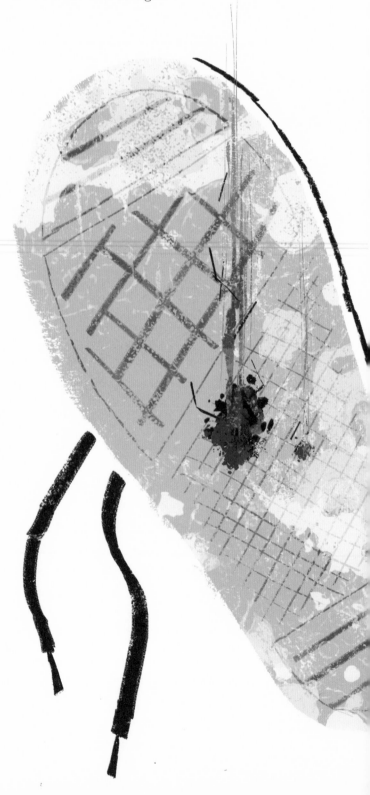

With the fly now fully imprisoned and paralyzed, the spider had one last step to prepare its meal. It plunged its fangs into the fly once more. Though unable to react, the fly could still feel the fiery pain as the fangs pumped digestive fluid into its body. The last thing the fly felt was its innards slowly dissolving into a soupy mess. The spider could now drink its meal directly from the fly's body, enough sustenance for perhaps a week.

The sun now hung low in the sky. The children had spent longer than they thought watching the fly's struggles. Their parents would be worried if they didn't get home soon. The group said its goodbyes and descended from the play structure, heading their separate directions across the playground.

The widow was nowhere to be seen; only her empty cart was left on the sidewalk. Wherever she had gone, the bulky mass she had been carrying had gone with her.

As the children left the mulch and headed for the sidewalk that surrounded the playground, they did not see the intricate network of thread the widow had left behind. As with any web, you couldn't see it until it was too late.

One by one the children ran into the thin threads that encircled them. At first, the webbing seemed a mere nuisance. They pulled at it, expecting it to come off. But grabbing at the thread only succeeded in further sticking them to the residue that coated the long thin strands. As the children pulled, twisted, and turned in the webbing the realization slowly set in. They were stuck.

128

It hadn't yet dawned on the children to look for the source of the webbing; they were still too frightened to do anything but struggle and call for help. If they had been searching, they might have looked into the trees above them.

There they would have found the black widow, now fully exposing her true form. Although hidden in the branches of the large trees overhead, she was gigantic. Ten feet long, she skittered and danced from branch to branch surveying her catch. Her pitch-black skin glinted in the setting sun.

As night fell on the playground, the widow positioned herself over her first prey. Of course the leader of this unruly gang of children would go first. She unsheathed her dripping fangs in preparation. Cruelty always found revenge, the widow mused as she emerged to a chorus of screams.

green eyes

Written by Jesse Reffsin
Illustrated by Chris Sasaki

Green Eyes

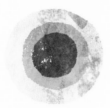

Teddy McNally was the new kid in school,
lonely and desperate for friends.
To get them he'd do whatever it took,
concerned not with means, but with ends.

One day in the halls, he heard a group talking,
some looking dreadful with fright.
They spoke of a set of ghostly green eyes
that came out in the graveyard at night.

Seeing his chance to seem brave and make friends
Teddy said he would seek out the eyes.
He asked for directions and received them in turn,
though the group thought his choice was unwise.

They told him to trek deep into the woods,
to find an old church made of stone.
Past the church was a wall and beyond that the graves,
set together yet each quite alone.

The moon must be absent to see the dead eyes
for the night must be colored pitch-black.
They'll come out at three, but make sure that you hide,
for if seen, you'll never come back.

With instructions in mind Teddy left that same night
for the crumbling church and its walls.
With no moon in the sky, he'd spot those green eyes,
then *he'd* be the talk of the halls.

The graveyard itself was a thing from the past,
each plot was a hundred years old.
The bodies they kept had been trapped there for years,
under dirt that lay heavy and cold.

As Teddy walked on past the graves that dark night,
he felt his own fear start to grow.
Though he tried to avoid it, his mind turned to thoughts
of the bodies that rotted below.

But he brushed off his fears and crouched by a grave.
The headstone had long since worn flat.
He was there for those eyes, those deathly green eyes,
so he kept his mind focused on that.

He waited in hiding till the hour was struck
and the church bell rang out three times.
Then he peeked from his stone and scanned the old place,
but the eyes had not come with the chimes.

And that's when it hit him—he felt he was watched.
He turned, wary of what he would find.
He peered through the dark with dread in his heart,
for the haunting green eyes were behind.

They were gruesome indeed as they bobbed there in place,
their stare hollow and cold as the night.
And then they lurched forward to where Teddy sat,
immobile with fear from the sight.

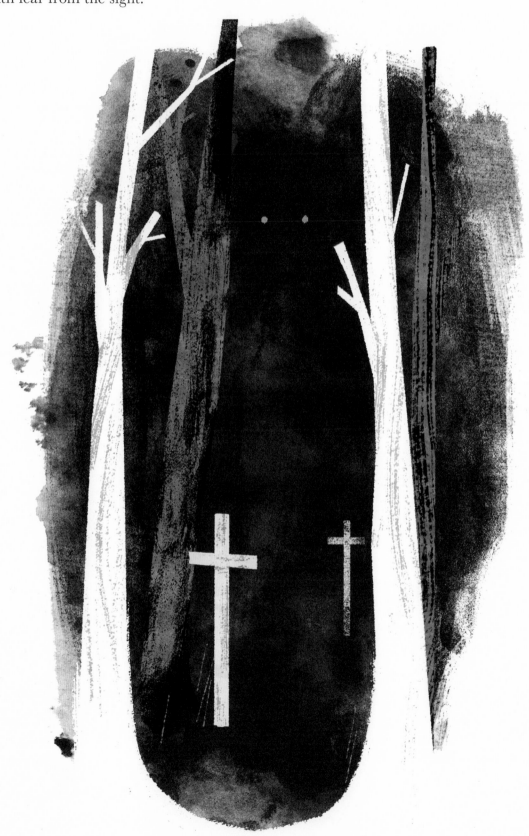

But as they moved toward him a body appeared,
its form filling in 'round the eyes.
A ghostly pale girl dressed in dirty white lace
now walked over to Teddy's surprise.

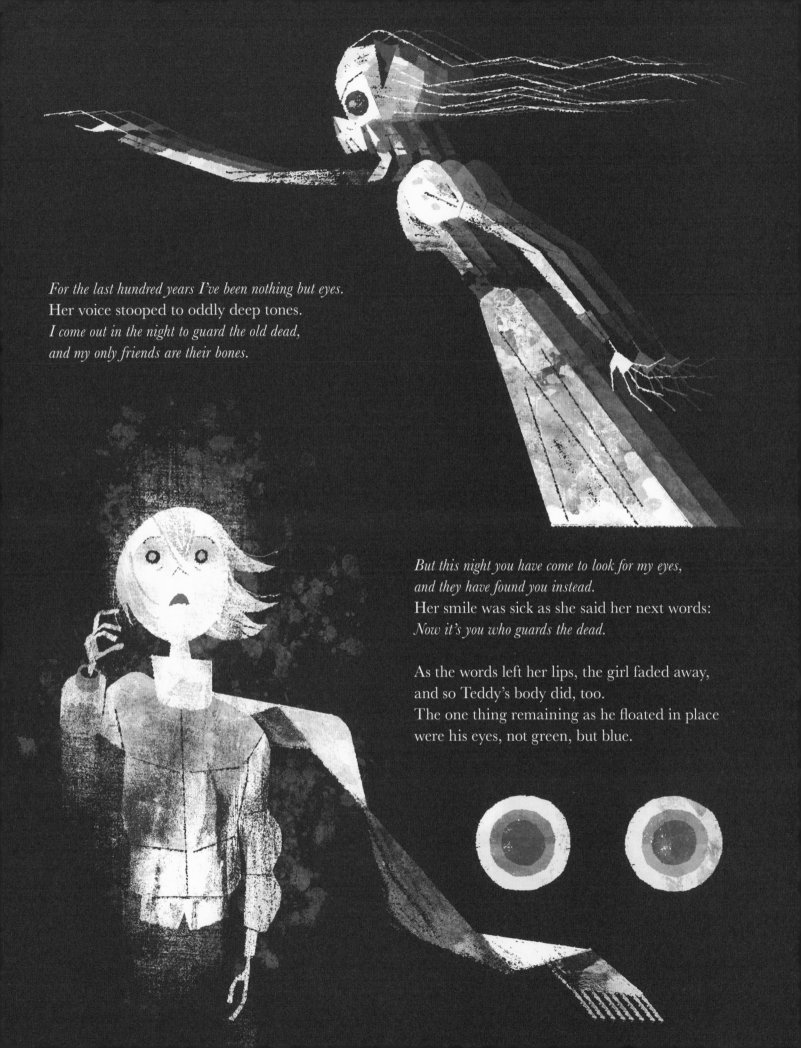

For the last hundred years I've been nothing but eyes.
Her voice stooped to oddly deep tones.
I come out in the night to guard the old dead,
and my only friends are their bones.

But this night you have come to look for my eyes,
and they have found you instead.
Her smile was sick as she said her next words:
Now it's you who guards the dead.

As the words left her lips, the girl faded away,
and so Teddy's body did, too.
The one thing remaining as he floated in place
were his eyes, not green, but blue.

And from that night forth he wandered the graves,
trapped by the old graveyard walls.
The friends he had found were the bones in the ground,
but at least blue eyes were the talk of the halls.

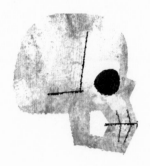

epilogue

Written by Blaise Hemingway
Illustrated by Jeff Turley

Epilogue

His stories now told, Old Man Blackwood leaned back into his chair and folded his arms over his chest, the hook on his prosthetic arm squeaking as it clasped open and closed.

Both Thomas and Skeeter stared back at him, their faces pale. They felt as if they'd had more than their share of the paranormal that night.

But as creepy as it all had been, surely the boys would be heroes when they returned to their cabins, rich with ghost stories from Old Man Blackwood himself. Thomas was certain that even the teenagers who worked in the mess hall would be impressed with his and Skeeter's daring.

"Thank you for telling us those stories, Mr. Blackwood," said Skeeter uneasily as he stood. "I guess we'll be off now."

"Wait," blurted Thomas. The boy thought back, counting the stories on his fingers. "It's only been twelve. He said there were thirteen true ghost stories, and he's only told us twelve."

"You see that, Skeeter? Thomas always pays attention," said Blackwood. "He catches that detail every time. You could learn something from him."

Thomas pushed away from the table. "I never said—we never told you our names."

Old Man Blackwood laughed, mucus crackling in his lungs as if about to erupt into a coughing fit. "Of course you did. You told me your names the first time you came to my cabin."

Thomas felt Skeeter tugging at his shirtsleeve, trying to pull him out of his seat. "Come on, Thomas. I wanna get out of here."

But Thomas refused to stand, grabbing hold of the table and locking eyes with Blackwood, who scratched his chin nonchalantly. "Sure," said Blackwood. "Run back to the camp. I'll just see you two back here tomorrow."

"Tell us the thirteenth ghost story," said Thomas insistently. "I wanna hear it."

"Stop talking that way to Old Man Black-wood," Skeeter whispered angrily. "You wanna end up being one of the skins on his walls!?!"

"You know, I always got a kick out of you kids calling me Old Man Blackwood back then." Blackwood smiled a little at a memory. "I was only thirty-five. I suppose that seems pretty old for a couple of twelve-year-olds."

"Tell us the thirteenth story!" Thomas repeated, this time more insistently.

"Come on, Thomas." Blackwood leaned forward to spit tobacco juice into his cup. "You already know the thirteenth story."

Thomas stared back into the chalky eyes of Old Man Blackwood as a memory slowly came to his mind like the first drops of a rain-storm. "That's it," said Blackwood, "you've got it."

Thomas spoke, slowly and methodically. "There were once two boys who snuck out of their bunks at midnight. They were hoping to hear a ghost story from the winter groundskeeper who lived on the outskirts of their camp."

Blackwood nodded as Thomas continued, *"But on the way*, the boys got stuck in the wet marsh mud and couldn't get free. They screamed and screamed, but they were too far away for anyone to hear them. That mud was like quicksand, and it slowly swallowed them."

Skeeter grabbed Thomas by the shoulders, shaking him. "That's enough, Thomas! Stop it! STOP IT!" But Thomas plodded ahead without emotion, his voice dying to a whisper.

"The camp was forced to close. It couldn't stay in business after the scandal of the two dead boys. *But* the groundskeeper remained in his little cabin, where every night, he is still visited by the ghosts of the two boys, who want to hear the thirteen true ghost stories, of which . . . their story is the last."

The End

about

Jeff Turley

Jeff Turley is a co-owner of Illustrátus as well as an Academy Award-winning production designer. He has a love for the outdoors and often wishes he was living in the woods with his wife, soaking in the fresh mountain air and enjoying all of God's creation.

Kit Turley

Kit Turley is a co-owner of Illustrátus and works in the production side of the animation and visual effects industries. When not making to-do lists and keeping things on schedule, Kit can be found cooking up a storm in the kitchen or walking her pup around Los Angeles.

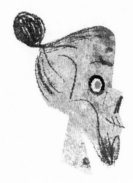

Chris Sasaki

Chris Sasaki is a character designer and illustrator living in Oakland, California. He works at Pixar Animation Studios and has designed characters for *Monsters University* and *Inside Out*. Most recently, he production designed the original short film, *Sanjay's Super Team*. *Ghost* is his first picture book.

Jesse Reffsin

Jesse Reffsin is a film and television writer based out of Los Angeles. When not at the beach or camping, he can be found in a dark closet working on his next horror or sci-fi project.

Blaise Hemingway

Blaise Hemingway writes for film and television and lives in Los Angeles with his wife, two kids, and semi-feral cat.

credits

Producer:
Kit Turley

Writers:
Blaise Hemingway
Jesse Reffsin

Illustrators:
Chris Sasaki
Jeff Turley

Layout Designer:
Pam Hsu

Additional Contributors:
Carol Manocchi-Verrino
Scott Turley

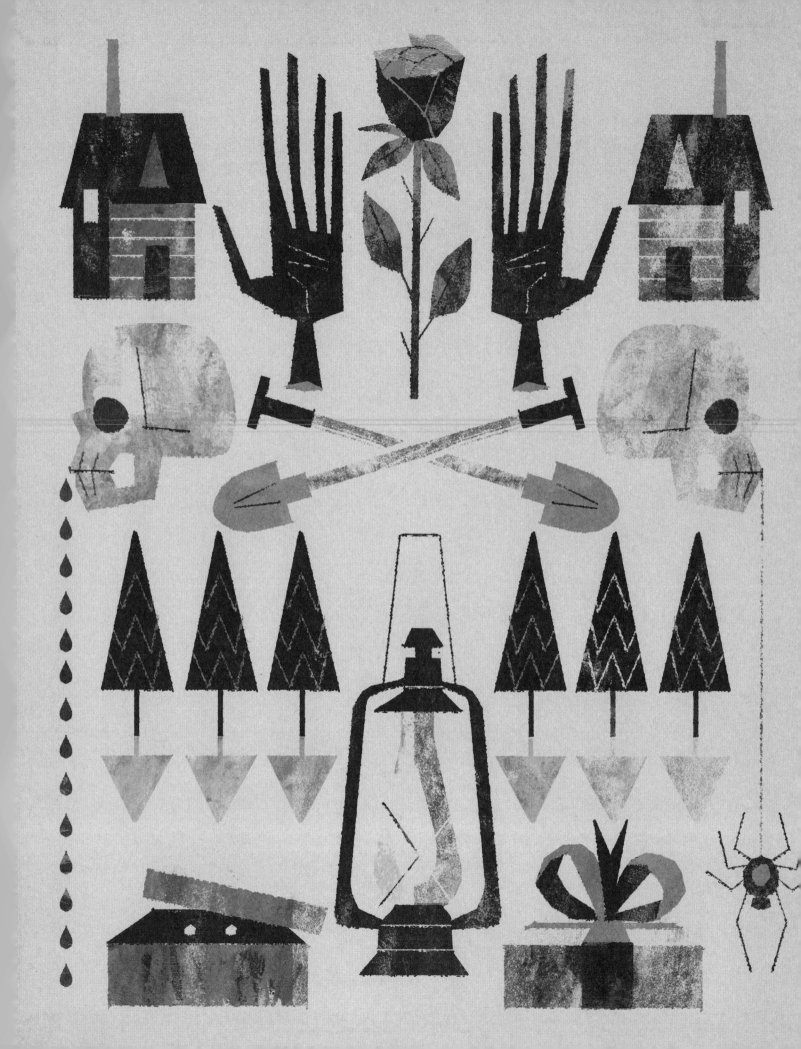